THE GUY

**A BEST FRIENDS
TO LOVERS
NOVELLA**

for Me

MARZY OPAL

The Guy For Me

Copyright © 2023 by Marzy Opal

Paperback ISBN: 978-1-7779123-8-3

Published by Marzy Opal
www.marzyopal.com

Editor: Emily A. Lawrence
Cover: Qamber Designs and Media W.L.L
Interior Formatting: Qamber Designs and Media W.L.L

WARNING

This book contains some strong language, sexual content, and mentions of bullying. Reader discretion is advised.

Please note: Montardor is a fictional city based in Central Canada.

For all the queens who love and empower others...

AUTHOR'S NOTE

Dear reader,

Thank you so much for picking up *The Guy For Me*. After I finished writing *Corrupted By You*, I needed a project that was lighter and sweeter. Mabel and Liam had been circling in my mind for quite some time until I finally sat down and penned their love story over the course of four months.

This is my first novella and it was such a fun experience to write about these two characters who are so utterly perfect for each other. They're gentle, kind, strong, and very lovable. I hope you adore them and enjoy their little journey towards a happily ever after.

As always, happy reading!

Love,

Marzy

PLAYLIST

Ariana Grande – Nasty
August Alsina – Don't Matter
Beyoncé – Alien Superstar
Beyoncé – Virgo's Groove
Chlöe – Have Mercy
DJ Khaled, Rihanna, Bryson Tiller – Wild Thoughts
Drake, Majid Jordan – Hold On, We're Going Home
Jhené Aiko – While We're Young
Khalid, Normani – Love Lies
Nicki Minaj ft. Ariana Grande – Bed
Selena Gomez – Good For You
Victoria Monét – Do You Like It
Zayn Malik – Let Me

PROLOGUE

Liam

For as long as I can remember, it's always been me, myself, and my solitude.

The same way we keep our enemies at arm's length, I've done so with the world. It's shown me its ugly sides more often than not, and I've spent a good chunk of my life hiding in its darkest corners to avoid being seen by my tormentors.

The problem with hiding?

Eventually, you are found.

And last week, I *was* found.

My entire body still hurts as a result. I feel like a walking, talking wound. Like someone gutted my insides and dissolved my bones, only to force me back together into a pitiful version of my once whole self.

Somehow, I find the strength to drag myself to first period English class. I sit in my usual seat in the back corner, close to the windows. Glancing out into the morning scenery gives me a reprieve. A moment to put my thoughts at bay and focus on the maple trees lining the school's courtyard. Fall is here. The leaves will start to change colours soon.

The bell rings and the sound is like a trigger. I close my eyes, suddenly remembering the blows I was dealt last week and how it inherently changed something inside of me. Taking the last bit of my softness and turning it into stone. Enticing me to turn my back forever on the people in this vicinity.

None of them were worth shit.

11

My teacher, Mrs. Fletcher, walks down the rows, handing out envelopes. I scrutinize the thick pile in her hands. Until I remember she mentioned starting an epistolary program with a teacher from another high school earlier this month.

Before last week, I was excited to pen my first letter to an anonymous recipient. Now I can't muster enough fucks to care.

It's funny; when you're in pain, nothing else registers in your mind. You'll go through the daily motions, but everything in your surroundings feels trivial. It all pales in comparison to the growing ache residing within you. A wound that refuses to heal.

Mrs. Fletcher smiles at me sympathetically and puts a hand on my shoulder, as if telling me she's proud I showed up today. Most of the faculty members are privy to what happened. Her gesture is meant to say *'Hang in there. It's all going to be okay.'*

I give her nothing but a blank stare in return.

She slips an envelope on my desk.

The next few minutes are a blur as she goes over the instructions. *Open your letter. Read it. This will be your pen pal for the next nine months. Pull out a blank loose leaf and write your response. Be courteous. Be kind. No bad words or rudeness, please. You have an hour to complete the task.*

There's not an enthusiastic bone in my body, but at least this mind-numbing exercise will give me something else to focus on besides my pain. I don't see any of the demon spawns responsible for my predicant, and that causes the tension coiled in my big shoulders to slowly ease away.

I gently open the envelope and take out the folded letter.

Cursive, feminine scrawl in blue ink greets me.

Dear friend,

It's so nice to 'meet' you. My name is Mabel and I'm a student in Mr. Johnson's class. Super stoked that we'll be pen pals for the next year!

A little bit about me: I just turned eighteen three weeks ago (fun fact: I share the same birthday as Beyoncé—September 4), I'm the tallest girl in my year (5'8"), I have a cat named Cheeto (she's literally orange like the snack), I'm trilingual (I speak English, French, and Tagalog) and I have a really big sweet tooth (white chocolate and Turon are my favourites). What about you? What are some of your favourite things? I'd love to know!

Mr. Johnson says the prompt for this letter is to discuss something we're looking forward to. If I'm being honest, I'm looking forward to finishing this school year and never looking back. High school is such a weird period in our lives, don't you agree? Some people peak. Others have barely blossomed. Some act like they're on top of the world, while others haven't even discovered their place in it. I kind of fall in the latter category. I have likes and dislikes. I have dreams and goals. I have a zest for life, but I'm not exactly sure where I'll end up in the future or where my place will be in the world. Is this something you can relate to?

Personally, the prospect of university has me quite excited. I'm ready to explore beyond the walls of Northwind High and make new friends—and not of the fake variety.

I want to submit an application to Vesta University's business school for the marketing program. I'm not sure if I'll have the grades to make it in. Or if I'll even fit in. But I'm super creative and I think it'll be a good way to apply myself. Are you planning on going to university next year and if so, what programs are you considering? Tell me everything, please. I'm so curious to know about you!

Oh, I also forgot to say that I'm really looking forward to the upcoming season of The Vampire Diaries *(If you haven't seen it yet, I regret to inform you this pen-pal-ship can't go any further). It's the best show ever and I will die on that hill. Another thing you should know about me: I'm obsessed with all things horror and supernatural. What kind of movies and TV shows do you like?*

Can't wait to hear from you. I hope you're doing well! 🌚

Sincerely,

Mabel

By the time I finish reading her letter, I have a genuine smile on my face. It hurts my split bottom lip, but I don't care. There's something about this girl that feels like a breath of fresh air. She seems kind, passionate, and funny enough, like a kindred soul.

I open my pencil case and pull out a matching blue ink pen.

Flexing my hand once to test my healing knuckles, I begin to write to her. Part of me wants to answer in a formal, cordial manner. Another part of me wants to hold nothing back.

I've given the right pieces of me to the wrong people and gotten hurt more times than I can count.

But as moments pass, I pen a letter just as enthusiastic to Mabel—a person who's done me no harm and simply wants to get to know me for the sake of this epistolary journey.

> *Dear Mabel,*
>
> *I hope this finds you well.*
>
> *It's really nice to 'meet' you too. My name is Liam.*
>
> *A little bit about me: I'm eighteen (it was actually my birthday this weekend), I'm the tallest guy in my year (6'5". Yes, I can practically imagine your eyes widening as you read this), I speak three languages as well (English, French— it's not the best, but I make do—and Irish, since I lived in Ireland until I turned eight years old), and just like you, I have a big sweet tooth. White chocolate happens to be my favourite as well and I'm quite fond of apple cake. I'll have to give* Turon *a try. What exactly is it and where can I find it?*
>
> *Will you believe me if I tell you that I'm also looking forward to finishing this year when it's only just begun? I fall in the latter category too, Mabel. I think high school should be a period of self-discovery to slowly equip you to deal with the real world once you graduate. We all have a place in the world. It'll just take some time to find it.*
>
> *Can I ask what some of your dreams and goals are?*
>
> *I read a quote once by Wayne Gretsky: "You miss one hundred percent of the shots you don't take." I firmly believe that you should apply to the marketing program. Study hard and have faith in yourself. I'm sure a few months from now you'll be holding your acceptance letter. Fingers crossed for you.*
>
> *I want to take a gap year to travel back to Ireland. My grandparents live there and I miss them very much. Once I return, I'd like to enroll in engineering. I've always liked to build things and I'm good with my hands.*
>
> *Speaking of Ireland, do you like to travel? If you've been anywhere cool, do tell.*
>
> *I have never seen* The Vampire Diaries, *but for the sake of upholding our ongoing pen-pal-ship, I'll try to binge-watch it this month. Similar to you, I like the horror/supernatural and action genres. My favourite movies are* X-men, Insidious, *and* The Silence of the Lambs. *I'm also an avid fantasy reader. Do you like books?*
>
> *It was really nice hearing from you, Mabel. Until next time!*
>
> *Sincerely,*
>
> *Liam*

I finish penning my letter. After reading it twice, I seal it in a new envelope that Mrs. Fletcher provides.

The smile stays on my face for the remainder of the day…and I realize that perhaps the rest of my school year won't suck.

Mabel and I continue exchanging correspondences for the next few months.

In each one, I unravel a new layer of this fascinating girl. I learn that she has a sad past—one that makes me want to punish the people who did her wrong—but I don't have the guts to tell her about mine. I share everything else, though.

All the pieces of me I'm proud of.

In every letter, we share our musings. No matter how inconsequential or paramount. Slowly, we relay all our dreams and life goals to each other. It's humbling to know that we have someone out there who'll always have our backs.

In the blink of an eye, Mabel and I become best friends.

We listen, motivate, and care for one another.

Mabel is my pillar and I'm hers.

Weeks later, I acknowledge the feeling moving in my chest every time I write to her or read one of her letters is the beginning spark of *love*.

She's the first person to have taken an actual interest in me and I lose myself in her.

Afraid of the outcome, I'm never able to echo those three little words.

I can't risk losing her friendship. I can't risk losing *her*.

So I keep the truth locked safely in my heart and choose to love her from afar.

Because guys like me don't get the happily ever after with girls like Mabel Garcia.

CHAPTER 1

Mabel

It's currently 8:00 p.m. on a Wednesday night and I'm at Marnie's Shack, a cute retro-themed dessert spot.

My best friend Kennedy is working the closing shift and the place is empty except for us two. Soft indie music pumps through the speakers as I sit by the pink bar with my MacBook in front of me, creating a Pinterest board for nail inspo.

Kennedy is behind the counter, preparing my drink. When she deposits it on a coaster, I inch her an appreciative grin. "Thanks, Ken."

We met during our freshmen year at Vesta University in business communication class and have been inseparable since. We're basically soul sisters.

"You're welcome." Kennedy tosses her dark box braids behind her shoulders with an adorable smile. "Are you still working on your assignment?"

"Nope. Finished and submitted four hours before the deadline." I'm a bit of a procrastinator and only started this assignment about… two hours ago. As the saying goes, diamonds are created under pressure and I'm confident that my one-thousand-word essay on 'How to create an effective personal brand' is nothing short of a masterpiece. Truly an A in the making. "Now I'm surfing through Pinterest to get ideas for my next set of nails. Any suggestions?"

She tilts her head and studies my current acrylics. I like my nails like I like my heels—long and lethal. "What do you think about yellow with some sunflowers?"

My nail technician is going to have a field day. "I love it. You're a genius."

She chuckles softly. "Oh, I know."

Kennedy is beauty and brains wrapped up in a silk designer bow. She's got the second highest GPA in Vesta University's business school and with deep brown skin, light brown eyes, and the kind of cheekbones that belong on a magazine cover, my best friend is easily the prettiest girl I've ever seen.

Before I can reply to her, my phone, which I forgot to switch to silent, buzzes with an incoming text message.

It's that *time* of the evening and even Kennedy knows, because she shoots me a shit-eating grin. "Who's that?"

I fight a blush. She knows damn well who it is.

There's only one person who texts me every day, without fail, at this time.

My other best friend.

Liam O'Connell.

When I was a senior in high school, my English teacher was super into epistolary writing and arranged for our class to have pen pals with another high school.

That's how Liam and I 'met' at eighteen.

Blue ink-stained letters filled with various musings, we found common ground in supernatural TV shows and the fact that we were both white chocolate lovers. Our relationship started on surface-level topics and morphed into something beyond our expectations.

He's someone with whom I can talk about everything and anything without the worry of being judged. There's no one like him.

He's patient, kind, and most of all, supportive.

Liam was the first person to know I got into the marketing program at Vesta University. He encouraged me to apply even when I was afraid my grades wouldn't measure up to the requirements.

When I got my first gig as a plus-size model for a popular Canadian lingerie brand a year ago, he was also the first person I texted. He celebrated my win like it was his own.

When I discussed wanting to start a social media account to spread body positivity and self-love, he was, once again, the first person to tell me I would make a difference in the world.

Even when I don't believe in myself, Liam believes in me.

And whenever I'm feeling down, stressed, or overall unhappy, he sends me a hefty money transfer so I can go get my nails done as a treat.

Essentially, I adore Liam with every fiber of my being.

He knows me like the back of his hand and besides Kennedy, he's the only person I trust.

Speaking of Kennedy, she's currently peering over, trying to get a look at my phone screen. "Are you texting your boyfriend?" she teases.

The word *boyfriend* associated with Liam causes butterflies to birth in my stomach.

"None of your business, Ken." I jokingly glare at her as I open his message.

How was your day, Bel? —Liam

I love that he calls me Bel. He's the only one who does. Everyone else uses May or Mabel. I like that he has something that's just for him.

Fantastic. Finished my assignment and picked my next set of nails —Bel

What have we decided on? —Liam

Yellow with sunflowers 😊 I'm repping team sunshine since you're a total grump. —Bel

Very cute, babe. —Liam

Every time he calls me babe (yes, I'm aware it's platonic), I melt into a puddle of mushy feelings.

Kennedy bursts my bubble of joy by asking, "Don't you think it's time you finally meet him in person, May?"

"Yeah." My shoulders deflate as I glance up at her. "I do think it's time."

Fun fact: I have no idea what Liam looks like.

After high school came to an end, we exchanged phone numbers in our last letter to keep in touch. But when I asked him to meet up, he said he was taking a gap year to visit his grandparents in Ireland. I even offered to video call because I was so desperate to see him, yet he dodged it with some lame excuse about the time difference.

For some reason, Liam has this need to remain hidden behind his walls.

Maybe the anonymity of our friendship makes it easier for him to open up. And I have a feeling someone has hurt Liam badly in the past, hence why he's a bit shy and reserved.

Except with me via text.

Maybe he also thinks that seeing each other will change things and ruin the magic?

Now that I'm in my sophomore year at Vesta University, our friendship has been going on for two years. And Liam is back in Montardor, which means we *have* to eventually meet.

We can't go on like this for much longer.

The urge to see him increases every time we text.

I may not know what Liam looks like, but once I do, it'll never change how I feel about him. I love his big heart and his golden soul, which shines with so much goodness.

Ignoring the odd pang travelling through my chest whenever I think of seeing Liam, I text him a picture of my mango milkshake.

If you had to drink one flavoured milkshake for the rest of your life, what would it be? —Bel

He replies within seconds.

Strawberry milkshake all the way. —Liam

Mango milkshake is the only acceptable answer. I'm contemplating our friendship. —Bel

One of my fondest childhood memories is eating mangoes with my *titas* (I'm half Filipina and that's how I address all my aunts on my dad's side) on hot summer evenings. I get my love for the fruit from them.

Then mango milkshake it is, babe. —Liam

There goes my heart, imagining fake scenarios with a best friend I have never seen. Imagining his looks, his height, his laugh, his smile, his eyes, and...you get the idea.

Kennedy gives me a meaningful look as she wipes the counter with a cloth. "So there's a mixer coming up this Friday. It's hosted by the Women in Business association at Vesta. We should go."

My thumbs stop moving on my phone screen and I arch an eyebrow. I was about to send Liam a funny GIF. "Uh, since when do I go out?"

It's sad, but I'm kind of an introvert. Along with my two friends, family, and cat, all I need are romance books, RnB music, and Disney movies to keep me happy.

"You never do, but don't you think it's time to leave the past in the past?" Ken bites her lip and gives me a gentle expression. "Things are different now."

My throat feels thick. It hurts to swallow.

Technically, things are different now.

But *how* different?

When I was a junior in high school, I went to a big party in South Side, Montardor, and met a charming, blond hockey player. He spent the night sweet-talking me and handing me drinks until I got shitfaced. When he said to meet him upstairs in one of the bedrooms to hook up, I remember being excited and desperate to get the awkward first time out of the way—to feel like an actual teenager for once—that I stumbled into the designated bedroom and waited for him in the dark.

I was such a fool thinking he was genuinely interested.

It was all a trap.

When he entered the room, we started kissing, only for me to realize it wasn't him but one of his hockey *teammates*...who he *roofied* and led to the room under the false pretense that I was his girlfriend. Both of us were blindsided and when the teammate's *real* girlfriend burst through the door, looking fifty shades of pissed and heartbroken, I figured out too late in my drunken stupor that I'd been roped into a revenge plot. One that had nothing to do with me and everything to do with the entitled rich kids of South Side, Montardor, who had no qualms about hurting others for their own gain.

That night gave birth to my trust issues and my dislike towards rich, blond boys who acted like the world belonged to them.

Although he did send me a letter of apology afterwards, the damage was already done.

After that party, I refused to go to large social gatherings. Nor do I drink alcohol in public.

Still, I appreciate Kennedy looking out for me and trying to get me to live a little.

"Where is this so-called mixer?" I deserve a medal for trying.

Kennedy twirls one of her braids between her fingers. "It's at MacGregor, the bar down the street. I think it could be a fun opportunity to kickstart the new semester and meet people."

I swallow the lump in my throat and slurp my mango milkshake. "What time is it at?"

"Nine p.m." Kennedy smiles hopefully. "Shannon switched shifts with me, so I'm not working closing time. I really want to go, May. Please?"

One bad experience shouldn't erase the possibility of new positive ones. Perhaps this is exactly what I need to step out of my comfort zone and try to expand my social circle. I'd probably feel less lonely in my upcoming classes if I actually made friends at this mixer.

"Okay. You're right. Let's do it." I use my silk scrunchie to tie my black hair—I was blond a while back before I dyed it back to my natural colour—into a ponytail. "I'll come pick you up at eight thirty."

"Oh my God. Do you really mean it?" Ken buzzes with excitement. "We're literally going to have such a good time."

If nothing comes of this, at least I made my best friend happy.

"Yeah, I'm down." I close my laptop and place it in my bag. "It might be fun."

"Why don't you ask Liam if he wants to come?"

My smile falters. "I guess...I could."

I mean, it won't hurt to ask him to the mixer, right? What's the worst that'll happen? He'll say no like always.

I tug up the strap of my bra—my tits, my favourite asset, give most bras a run for their money—and pull up Liam's conversation. Before I can chicken out, I shoot my shot.

What are you doing this Friday? —Bel

Liam replies instantly. He never makes me wait long.

What's happening Friday? —Liam

There's this mixer at MacGregor. Kennedy convinced me to go and I think it might be fun. Wanna join? —Bel

I hold my breath, awaiting his response. Every second stretches into an eternity when you're anticipating something. Shit. I'm sweating. Under boobs. Under arms. Under whatever you name it. I practically finish my milkshake in two more slurps.

Maybe I'll meet you there. —Liam

I blink a few times.

Really? —Bel

Yeah. I'll text you Friday to confirm. —Liam

Holy moly. Am I finally going to meet my pen-pal-turned-text-best-friend?

Common sense tells me not to get too excited. This is Liam. King of all flakers. King of excuses. King of *Let's-get-Mabel's-hopes-high-for-no-goddamn-reason.*

But my hopeless heart doesn't get the memo as I text back.

Perfect ☺ I can't wait to see you <3. —Be

CHAPTER 2

Mabel

> I can't make it, Bel. I'm so sorry. Something came up.
> —Liam

To say Liam's latest text put a damper on my mood is an understatement.

I just remembered why I don't date. Men are confusing as hell and only good for one thing: opening jars. Considering most of them can't even locate the clit, I stand firm in my previous statement.

I can smell bullshit from a mile away. If Liam doesn't want to see me, fine. Doesn't mean I'm not going to give him the cold shoulder for twenty-four hours. We never fight. Rarely argue unless it's over trivial things like the best horror movie, the best spot for summer vacationing, and the best boyband in the world. *The Silence of the Lambs*, Seychelles, and One Direction are the only acceptable answers, by the way.

But this straight-up annoys me.

Once again, I built my hopes up for nothing. The only thing keeping me going this week was the fact that I was going to meet Liam in person.

I got a new outfit. I got my nails done. I got my pussy Brazilian waxed and for what? For Liam to bail on me!

I finally experience the worldwide disappointment girls feel when their dick appointments cancel on them. Not that this was a dick appointment, but it did involve a frustrating guy who has a dick, so yeah, you get the gist of it.

I leave Liam on read and text Kennedy.

I'm leaving in ten minutes to pick you up. —May

Kennedy replies to my text with a simple thumbs-up.

My cat, Cheeto, snuggles up to my feet. I bend down to pick her up and nuzzle her orange fur. She paws at my hair before comfortably settling against my chest.

"Stay away from boys, Cheeto," I whisper to her and she blinks her big eyes at me. "They're useless. Repeat after me. No boys. Ever."

Cheeto meows in response.

"That's good enough." I lower her to the foot of my bed and she stretches out. "And stop playing with the neighbour's cat. I know he fancies you. Next thing you know, you'll get your kitty ass knocked up. Got it?"

Cheeto can't be bothered with me. She meows again and I sigh, walking over to my full-length mirror.

Nerves have my belly in a knot. Obviously, I know this is great for me. Getting out. Meeting new people. Expanding my horizons. Yada. Yada. Yada. Dipping my toes in the social scene is a lot like dipping my toes in the dating pool: lacking luster and so unnecessary when I already have a small circle of people who adore me and who I adore in return.

But alas, we are doing this.

I glance at my reflection in the mirror.

Having spent so much of my time in photoshoots with a caked-on face, I keep my makeup minimal today with foundation, mascara, and some pink-tinted lip gloss. I've straightened my hair and donned an off-the-shoulder black top, black denim skirt, and black stilettos that can *cut*.

I can confidently say I look good.

Despite the blemish slightly visible on my cheek. Despite the light cellulite on my upper thighs. Despite the fact that some would deem I need to shed a few pounds before being the perfect weight.

Social media has women of all ages criticizing and comparing themselves to unrealistic standards, unfortunately. Self-love is a tough journey, but it's one worth taking because the end result—living comfortably in your skin and experiencing true happiness—is absolutely wondrous.

It took me years to come to this powerful realization: I am essentially perfect. It's society that is not.

The only thing missing to make me *feel* perfect in this moment is a smile on my face.

Which refuses to show up now that Liam isn't going to be there.

As always, I snap a picture of myself in my full-length mirror, making sure to showcase my killer heels, and post it on my Instagram account with the hashtag 'OOTD.' Within seconds, I'm flooded by likes and empowering comments.

It helps ease the sting of being stood up.

After responding to a few comments, I throw on my small crossbody purse and walk out.

Time to go have fun.

I'm not having fun at all.

The inside of MacGregor feels like an oven and even the air is saturated with a myriad of smells: two-dollar tequila shots, cheap perfume, and horrendous BO.

The music is too loud and we're packed in like sardines. Currently, Kennedy and I are squeezed between two sorority sisters, who're drinking liquor like it's water and giving every man a run for his money. As they totally should.

"Can we leave?" I holler in Kennedy's ear, hoping she'll hear me over the ruckus.

"It's only been twenty minutes, May!" she hollers back.

Twenty minutes of me *trying*. That's got to count for something.

I put on my best pleading face. "Please, Ken."

Kennedy smiles like a good sport instead of getting aggravated by my introvertedness. Is that a word? I'm making it one. "How about we stay another forty minutes and then we can grab gelato from the new place that opened up downtown?"

"Deal." The way to my heart is truly through food.

"I'm really happy we came out tonight." Kennedy throws her arms around me in a crushing hug. She may be small, but she's freakishly strong. "C'mon, let's get drinks!"

Clearly, she's enjoying tonight.

Me and my under-boob sweat really are not.

I envy how cool and collected Kennedy appears. Not a single rivulet of sweat on her skin.

My best friend looks super cute in a blazer dress. Tonight her palette is a pretty green and she's gracefully adorned in dainty gold jewellery. If there was one way to describe Kennedy's style, it would be business chic. This girl owns a blazer in every single colour of the rainbow and heels to match them.

I've noticed a bunch of guys eyeing her, but she pays them no mind as she orders our drinks. Sex on the beach for her and a Shirley Temple for me.

We clink our glasses together. "Cheers to—"

Kennedy's words hang in the air as she spots something over my shoulder.

Frowning, I follow her line of vision.

A devious grin curls my lips.

She's gazing at the billiard tables, where a bunch of guys from Vesta University are gathered. One of the guys from the crew glances up and sees Ken.

Caleb Wright.

Hockey playing business bro. Kind of a playboy (he gets around, if all the gossip around the school is correct). Body and face totally fitting for male underwear ads.

And also known as Kennedy's crush.

Now it all makes sense.

I try to keep the teasing to a minimum but fail, of course. "So *this* is why you wanted to come out tonight. You knew Caleb would be here."

Kennedy actually blushes. "I have no idea what you're talking about."

Here's the thing. My best friend has been infatuated with this guy for as long as I can remember. She's never had the guts to make the first move and neither has he, for that matter. But I'm willing to bet he's just as attracted to her, if not more.

Maybe tonight they can stop playing the cat-and-mouse game and finally get together.

Caleb's lips twist in a cocky smirk. He leans against the wall and crosses his arms, perusing her from top to bottom. The invitation is clear as day. He's basically eye-fucking Kennedy and saying *give it to me*.

I lightly shove her shoulder. "Men are the weakest link. If a woman wants anything done, she needs to take initiative herself. Go make the first move and for God's sake, slice the sexual tension. It's giving me hives."

Kennedy releases a choked chuckle. "I can't believe you said that."

"Believe it. Now go! Otherwise, I'm going to carry you there myself cavewoman-style and lay you at his feet like an offering, Ken. Don't make me embarrass us both tonight."

She knows I'm not kidding.

Kennedy gathers liquid courage by tossing back her drink. "Okay. I'm doing it. How do I look?"

"Like a million bucks."

She cracks a smile filled with gratitude. "In case I haven't said it today, I love you."

"I know you do. Now channel your inner lioness and show Caleb what he's missing."

"Right. I can do this." She nods adamantly, tucking her braids behind her ear. "Lioness. That's what I am. Hear me roar."

"Atta girl." I slap her ass to get her moving in the right direction.

I watch like a proud mama as Kennedy sashays towards Caleb with all the confidence of a siren, her hips swaying with every step. He watches her like an arrogant man who's already whipped.

As I guzzle down my Shirley Temple, I notice two girls approaching me from my peripheral vision. They have hopeful, tentative expressions as they ask, "Are you Mabel?"

Confused, I reply politely, "Yes, that's me."

Maybe we've shared classes in the past?

One of the girls breaks out in excitement. "We knew you looked familiar."

In the span of five minutes, I learn they follow my Instagram at *mabelgarciaxo*. They recognized me and wanted to come say hello. I have nearly seventy thousand followers and my social media account is all about being a self-loving plus-sized model slash university student trying to inspire women to live their truth and be more confident.

The girls tell me how much they appreciate the message I'm broadcasting and the way my posts have inspired them.

Warmth fills my chest and I stand there stunned.

Sometimes we momentarily forget our own worth until someone reminds us. It's so easy to get lost in an ever-churning pit of self-deprecation and bad thoughts. But moments like these pull you back to the surface and ground you.

A conversation on society's beauty standards ensues. We talk about the ways to unlearn the concepts that harm us, while learning to unconditionally love the skin we're in.

When we wrap up, I follow the girls back on Instagram and they leave with friendly waves and a bounce to their steps. I'm thankful I came out tonight and stepped out of my comfort zone, if only for this one sweet interaction. Socializing with them was a good reminder that not everyone is malicious and out to get me for their own benefit.

The feeling of cloud nine evaporates when I glance over at Kennedy and Caleb, who're having the time of their lives flirting openly in a crowded bar.

Suddenly, all I can think about is Liam.

A score of emotions rushes through my system.

Elation that I came out. Disappointment that Liam flaked on me.

Needing a moment away from the music and chatter, I thread through the crowd towards the bathrooms tucked in the back corridor.

Lady luck must hate me.

Before I even make it three steps, a tall dude manages to sock my cheekbone with his flailing elbow as he does the chicken dance to impress the girl next to him.

There's a sickening sound as skin slaps skin and we both gasp out loud.

Him, out of fear. Me, out of shock, because I've literally been skyrocketed to a whole new dimension.

Excruciating pain explodes over my nerve endings and I sway.

The contents of my Shirley Temple splash all over the ground in a sticky mess, causing a few people to shriek.

"I'm so s-sorry," I choke out to no one in particular.

A loud commotion occurs as people shuffle away. My cheeks heat up with scorching humiliation.

The taunting voice in my head whispers condescendingly, *See, Mabel? This is why you don't go out. Something embarrassing always happens to you. Should have stayed at home with Cheeto watching movies.*

The guy who smacked me is profusely apologizing, but I'm too busy holding my cheek, wallowing in self-pity, to reply back.

Out of the blue, a deep voice booms, "Move out of the way!"

Jolting, I glance up…and instantly freeze.

There's only one way to describe the man entering my line of sight.

Tall, handsome, and just the perfect amount of rugged.

He looks like a real-life warrior.

His hair is brown with tinges of auburn, cropped short at the side, with the longer strands at the top a bit dishevelled. Like he combed his fingers through it and now it's just doing its own thing.

And his body.

Lord have mercy.

He's strong and thick, and his husky frame is poured in the customary black polo and dark denim of MacGregor's bouncers. I swear my mouth waters at the sight of those bulging muscles and the way they flex as he pushes people aside to get to me.

His features are twisted in a scowl, and I see his jaw clench beneath his full beard as he stands before me, inspecting my frame from head to toe.

Those blue eyes of his, turbulent like the ocean, are ablaze.

And when our gazes collide, I swear the world stops spinning on its axis for a moment.

CHAPTER 3

Liam

Well, if it isn't the girl of my dreams.

Jesus Christ.

She's so beautiful, I'm stunned.

I was already in love with my best friend, but seeing her in person? I'm completely obsessed.

Silky black hair down to her waist. Brown eyes framed by dark lashes. Pouty lips, glossed to perfection. Heart-shaped face that I just want to cup and see if her tan skin feels as soft as it looks.

My throat goes dry when I notice the little black outfit wrapped around her curves. Seeing her bountiful cleavage has me feeling like one of Pavlov's dogs. Not to mention that I want those sexy heels-clad feet resting over my shoulders as I, respectfully, fuck us both six ways to Sunday.

Mabel Garcia has been the object of my love and affection for two years. She has no idea how often I've stared at her pictures and memorized every detail so that I can close my eyes and imagine her vividly. She has no idea that our first meeting makes my heart feel like it's been struck by an arrow.

The girl of my dreams has no idea that she looks like a goddess and I feel like a humble servant ready to worship at her altar.

Mabel has never seen me in person or pictures; it's not like she can recognize me.

But some part of me wishes, as she stares up at my face, that she realizes it's *me*.

Her best friend.

Her Liam.

Suddenly, guilt pricks my conscience. I got her hopes up by saying I might meet her, then bailed like a coward because one, I wasn't ready to face her and two, I ended up having to work tonight's shift.

My mind drifts back to earth. I remember that we're in MacGregor, surrounded by a lot of bargoers, and Mabel is cradling her cheek. She just got elbowed in the face by a little shit who has no sense of direction.

Anger pulses in my frame. I grab the guy—who accidentally hit her— by the scruff of the neck. He's still apologizing when I push him in the opposite direction of her, where he can't do any more damage.

As a bouncer, it's my job to break up 'incidents' like these. Though it's not every day that it involves the girl you love. I try to separate my personal feelings to not give away too much, but I still end up snarling, "Get the fuck out of here!"

The crowd disperses with one heated look from me.

Mabel is still rooted to her spot when I turn back to face her.

I take a step closer to her.

At six-five, I tower over everyone, but Mabel in her heels reaches my chest. She doesn't seem intimidated by my giant stature. A rare occurrence since most people scurry away in my proximity.

She actually stares at me with a mixture of awe and wonderment.

It's all the courage I need to dip my head and urge in a low voice, "Are you okay?"

We're almost eye-level now. She nods, almost shyly. "Uh, yes. Thank you for…that."

"You don't have to thank me," I rasp, my fingers flexing. Wanting to reach for her cheek to soothe her. I stop myself because that would be creepy considering we just 'met.' "That looks really rough."

"It feels like it too." She lets out a self-deprecating laugh and mumbles under her breath, "That's what I get for stepping out of my comfort zone."

I'm not sure I understand what she means. All I know is a nasty bruise is forming and I can't stand to see it on her gorgeous skin. I grind my jaw. "Listen, I can get you some ice from the bar. It should help with the swelling."

She's not embarrassed anymore, as the people around us have already forgotten about the commotion and gone back to partying. But her shoulders still sag and I hate the overall sadness swirling around her. "Yeah, I guess that would be nice."

"Okay, follow me." I whirl around to pave our way, then stop short, throwing her a quick glance over my shoulder. "I'm Lee, by the way."

Mabel has only ever called me Liam, so Lee is a safe enough nickname. She won't have an inkling it's me and honestly, I don't want her to.

It's pathetic to say out loud, but I'm a bit of an insecure jackass.

I don't necessarily like what I see in the mirror, but I've made peace with my looks, height and…weight. I know I'm not conventionally handsome. At least I'm physically stronger than most. Growing up, I've always been an outcast due to my appearance. While Mabel isn't the judgy kind, I don't want to disappoint her.

She's so out of my league, it's not even funny.

Mabel's this smart, kind, and beautiful girl.

And I'm, well, *me*.

I have an impeccable work ethic, I care for the people I love, and I'm a gentleman where it matters, but my head's not so far up my ass to assume someone like her would want to have a romantic relationship with me.

She probably thinks her text best friend is some lean, normal-sized dude. Not a giant-sized guy who looks like an ugly bruiser.

The thought irritates me, yet the feeling is short-lived when Mabel smiles at me. "Nice to meet you, Lee. I'm May."

Her smile lights up my insides like a Christmas tree.

God, she's so lovely it actually hurts.

I get a kick out of her not introducing herself as Bel. That's my nickname for her and I'm a territorial motherfucker. I'd hate to know strangers get to call her Bel.

I know, I know. How very caveman of me.

Giving her a tentative smile of my own, I say, "Likewise, May."

We thread our way through the thick crowd. I want to grab her hand, but I don't because she didn't consent to it. She still follows closely behind, her presence warming my back like the sun after days of rain.

That's what Mabel is to me. My little sunshine in my otherwise gloomy life.

We reach the busy bar and I signal the bartender. Pia catches my eyes and saunters over despite the numerous order calls. "What's up?"

"I need some ice." I chin nod towards the cash register. There's a small bowl filled with individually wrapped white chocolate truffles. We keep them to snack on during our shifts. They also happen to be Mabel's and my favourites. "And a handful of those."

Pia, bless her heart, hands me the entire bowl along with a plastic cup filled with ice. "Everything okay?"

When Pia spots Mabel standing behind me, her eyes widen with recognition.

Besides Mabel, Pia is the other friend I'm closest to. As a result, I've told her about my secret crush. I'm notorious for scrolling through Mabel's Instagram in the staff breakroom and Pia has seen me hopelessly pine over the sexy minx of a model on multiple occasions.

Pitiful, maybe, but I have zero regrets.

I can stare at Mabel all day long and not get bored.

"Listen, I'm taking my break now. Let Donovan know if he asks, all right?"

"Sounds good." Pia gives me a wink before going back to making drinks. I already know when the night is over, she's going to demand a play-by-play.

Always rooting for the underdog, Pia is my biggest cheerleader.

When I turn back to Mabel, she stares up at me with this softness that twists my insides. All at once, I want to get into her mind and see what she sees when she looks at me.

"Thank you." She shifts on her heels. "For getting me ice. That was kind of you."

The music is too loud. I crane my head down and say close to her ear, "I know a place in the back where we can sit down and nurse your bruise. Would you like to go with me?"

I'm certain she came here with her best friend Kennedy, who is nowhere to be seen. I'm hoping Mabel will want my company in the meantime.

"Yes, please."

My chest puffs with pride and I lead us to the back of the bar, near the emergency exit. There's a brick-walled hallway lined with a wooden bench where the staff sometimes relaxes. We keep the back door open for fresh air too, so there's a nice breeze when Mabel and I arrive in the dimly lit space.

She's the first to lower herself onto the bench and I follow suit, keeping a decent amount of distance between us. I hand her the plastic cup and the ice cubes clink together.

Mabel places it against her cheek and hisses a little. "Ouch."

Accident or not, the urge to beat up the guy who hit her returns. "That'll take down the swelling and it shouldn't be too bad by tomorrow."

She sighs heavily. "I hope so. I have a photoshoot in a few days and I can't afford to have a big bruise on my cheek."

I crack my tattooed knuckles. I know that Mabel works as a part-time model while being a marketing student. My girl's a hustler. Another thing I love about her.

"What kind of photoshoot?" I ask as if I don't have a clue. Anything to hear her soft, raspy voice again.

She stretches her bronzed legs out and her black skirt rides higher up her thick thighs. I stifle a groan, the mental image of them splayed open as I drizzle gentle kisses searing into my mind.

No one turns me on like this woman.

My phone is filled with spank bank material of Mabel, various shots straight from her Instagram. A few months ago, she did a swimsuit photoshoot and I nearly lost my mind seeing her wet in a little yellow bikini that *barely* contained anything.

It's my favourite thing to look at every night before bed.

"It's a lingerie photoshoot. I actually work as a model."

I stretch my legs out too. "Ah, I see. Do you enjoy what you do?"

A light twinkles in Mabel's eyes. "Some days are very long and exhausting, but yes, I love what I do. I know my angles and I feel my most confident in front of a camera. For me, modelling is a very empowering experience."

That much is obvious. Her passion shines through in every picture she posts. I wish I can tell her in person—and not text—how proud I am of her.

"That's amazing, May," I say instead, my voice gruff and sincere.

"Thanks for helping me out." Her brown eyes meet mine and her smile morphs into a grin. "You also didn't have to hang out with me while I ice this."

I only ever want to be where you are, sweetheart.

I shrug my shoulders like it's no big deal, but this feels like the most defining moment of my life. I want to pinch myself. However, if this is a dream, I never want to wake up.

"I was going on break anyway, and I'm not very fond of loud places."

"Ironic, considering where you work, eh?" I love that she's teasing me. "I'm not a fan of big gatherings either. I came here as a favour for a friend."

I know why Mabel doesn't like big gatherings. The thought of what happened to her in the past makes my blood boil. Some shitty person really decided to mess with my girl for his own benefit and it pains me that it's left Mabel with this kind of trauma.

"Where is your friend now?"

"Hopefully getting it on with her crush. Figured I'd give them some alone time before I cockblock."

Silence falls upon us. It's not strenuous, though. More companionable. My inability to open up to others except for Mabel and Pia has made me a bit of a loner. Which is fine with me since most people suck anyways.

I've learned in life that people are rarely interested in you unless they can benefit from you in some way. And when you no longer serve their purpose, they'll toss you away like yesterday's trash.

Except for Bel.

During the epistolary writing program, Mabel cared about me when no one else did. She made me feel like I was more than an object for others' entertainment—like I had a voice. Because she'd never seen me, to her I wasn't the guy who was bullied for his size. Or the one the mean girls at school asked out as a sick joke just so they could humiliate me in front of the popular kids.

To Bel, I was just me.

Liam O'Connell, the guy who enjoyed watching action and cult classic horror films, who liked gardening on the weekend with his mother, who loved reading fantasy novels, and who dreamed of building all sorts of creations straight from his imagination.

To her, I *mattered*.

Falling in love with my best friend was inevitable and it happened within weeks of knowing her.

Mabel has owned me from the first letter and she continues to own me, even after two years.

I push the bowl of white chocolate truffles down the bench after taking one myself. "Here. Help yourself."

She watches me unwrap one and plop it into my mouth before

mimicking me. "White chocolate is my favourite."

I know. "Mine too."

We share a secret smile.

"So, Lee. Tell me about yourself." Mabel practically moans when the chocolate hits her palate and I shift uncomfortably, my semi stiff against the seam of my dark jeans.

That sound is like music to my ears.

"What would you like to know?" I barely manage to utter the words.

"How old are you?" She reaches for another chocolate. Pride soars through me when I notice the nails with sunflowers on them. Mabel sent me pictures last night after getting them done. I love seeing her wear something I helped provide for.

I'm picturing those nails raking down my back like a total bastard. Everything I've felt for this girl in the last two years is magnified now that she's physically in my vicinity. I'm feeling horny, happy, and so damn in love.

"I'm twenty." I almost choke on my saliva when Mabel licks the melted white chocolate off her thumb like a fucking dicktease.

"No kidding. Same. What else do you do besides rescuing damsels in distress?"

That makes me laugh. "Besides rescuing damsels in distress, I go to school. I'm studying engineering."

I'm nervous for a second. It feels like Mabel can see right through me—see that I'm *Liam*. I deliberately avoid saying which kind of engineering since she knows I'm studying civil. Not to mention, I've lied to her in the past and said I studied at another institute. I was worried if I said Vesta University, she'd scope out the entire place until she found me.

I've never been ready to be physically found by her, but tonight? I'm considering telling her the truth about my identity.

I've played out the scenario of us meeting for the first time in my mind often. In all of them, Mabel looks horrified at my hefty appearance and the light scar that cuts over my cheek, half hidden beneath my beard.

Except right now she's far from horrified. Dare I say, she appears pretty comfortable and relaxed. Maybe learning that I'm Liam won't be so bad after all.

She'll be annoyed that I lied, but I don't think she'll toss me aside like a defective toy...

"Nice. What would you like to do in that field?" She adjusts the shoulders of her top and her cleavage bounces.

I've died and gone to heaven.

"Engineering is quite vast and there's a lot I can do in it." I redirect my gaze to the ground before she catches me staring at her. "But I know for certain I like working with my hands since I've always been passionate about building things from scratch."

One of my long-term goals is to be able to work as a construction manager, overseeing projects from start to finish. The idea of one day walking on a bridge or standing in a building I helped build is a fascinating concept to me.

Mabel crosses her legs and angles her body my way, giving me her full attention. Like she's genuinely interested in me. "What kind of things do you like to build?"

Now's probably a bad time to tell her I built her a desk after she complained about needing a new one three weeks ago. It's white and solid wood to match her room's aesthetic. I was going to gather the courage to ask her for her address so I could drop it off in the next few days.

"Anything I can build. I don't limit myself. I started with making bird houses and eventually worked my way up to things like bed frames, dressers...office desks."

Her jaw slackens. She's extremely impressed. My cheeks heat up.

"That's really amazing, Lee. Most people live their whole lives without figuring out what they're meant to do and I think there's something powerful in finding your passion and pursuing it." Is she getting closer to me or is that my starved imagination conjuring up this whole thing? "Who knows, maybe you'll build the world's eighth wonder one day."

That makes me chuckle too. This girl. She just gets me. "Who knows, eh? Maybe I'll even name it after you."

Don't ask me where I got the balls to flirt with that one-liner. It's the godawful truth, though. If I could ever build something so grand as another wonder, I'd name it after her.

Mabel winks, flirting back. "Very much appreciated."

She reaches for another white chocolate and hands me one. I take it and our fingers brush. I think my heart skipped a beat. "How is your cheek feeling?"

Mabel touches the tender spot and sighs. "It's fine. Nothing some good concealer and colour correcting can't fix."

The ice is practically melted in the cup. I gesture with my hand for her to give it. She does and I set it down on the far side of the bench where we won't accidentally knock it over.

When I turn my attention back to her, she's staring at my tattoos.

"Can I?" Mabel asks, biting her bottom lip.

I nod and she slides down the bench until our thighs are nearly touching. My heart is now in overdrive, dancing with pure happiness.

"Wow." Her fingers feather over my right arm, tracing the sword. Most of my tattoos represent symbols from my favourite novels. "It's so intricate and beautiful."

"Thank you." I shiver at her gentle touch.

Grabbing my left wrist, she extends my arm and gazes at the scenic landscape of a fictional world. She marvels over the detailing.

The low light above our heads casts an angelic glow over Mabel's face as she concentrates on my art. Her brows knit and her lips pucker in an endearing manner.

When a curtain of her dark hair falls forward as she leans in to get a better look, I'm helpless to tuck it behind her ear.

A shot of electricity crackles between us and Mabel gasps, lifting her head.

My own inhale is sharp.

We're mere centimeters away from each other, breathing the same air. It's exhilarating.

"You're so…beautiful," I murmur, my tone timid. "I wanted to tell you when I first saw you." With my free hand, I gently cup her face and skim the pad of my thumb over her cheek. "Took my breath away, Bel."

Mabel's eyes soften, her lips parting. "Lee…"

She's still holding my wrist in her hand. There's no doubt she can feel how fast my pulse beats.

For her.

Always.

Then something causes her expression to scrunch and she says accusingly, "What did you just call me?"

Oh, fuck.

CHAPTER 4

Mabel

I'm not crazy.

I swear I heard it.

Bel.

Only one guy calls me that.

Lee drops the hand holding my face like it catches fire. His Adam's apple works with a nervous swallow. "I-I said you're beautiful."

The butterflies swarming in my stomach from his compliment suddenly evaporate.

There was a sense of ease when I was talking to Lee—like I just *knew* him from somewhere. Of course, I felt an irresistible attraction from the second I laid my eyes on him, but there was something more. I couldn't place my finger on it until now…

"No. No." I scurry back on the bench, creating distance between us. "You called me *Bel*."

I introduced myself as May. Not Mabel. And certainly not Bel.

"Listen, May, I—"

A final cog clicks in my mind. Before he can complete his sentence, I grab his left hand and twist it around so I can see his thumb.

I glare at the solid font tattoo that's etched there in black ink.

IV

Liam got the roman numeral tatted a few months ago and sent me a picture of it. He said it was a tribute to me since I was born on the fourth of September and his tattoos were meant to showcase his favourite things and memories.

I'd recognize that tattoo anywhere. I've memorized it wholly. I cried when I first saw it. There was someone out there who treasured me so much that a piece of me was inked on their skin forever. I couldn't believe it. My heart had nearly burst out of my chest.

Now I'm saved from addressing the elephant in the room when the bartender from earlier enters the quiet hallway. "Hey, Donovan is looking for you, Liam—"

Her sentence hangs in the air when she spots us sitting next to each other in stunned silence.

My suspicions are confirmed.

Liam.

The guy in front of me is not some bouncer I met at a bar on a chance encounter and flirted with harmlessly.

No.

The guy in front of me is *my* best friend Liam.

"Liam?" I echo.

Liam's skin has gone a ghostly pale. He still isn't looking at me, his eyes fixed on the bartender as they engage in a staring contest that screams *you've-really-fucked-up.*

"Your name is Liam." It's not a question. It's a fucking statement.

Something seems to dawn on the bartender and she lets out a low exhale. "Oh, shit. I wasn't supposed to say anything."

Liam's eyes close with a hint of defeat.

I've gone a little numb with shock.

"I, uh, I'm going to go now." She cringes and scratches her pixie cut awkwardly. "Sorry for disturbing."

She stumbles away with an apologetic glance.

Now it's just Liam and me left, and this newfound revelation hanging over our heads like a bad omen.

The happiness at finally having what I want—seeing my best friend in person—is quickly overshadowed by the disappointment of him lying to me about his identity.

"Liam." I hate the frail quality of my voice. "Why...didn't you tell me it was you?"

His blue eyes spell out his misery. "Because I didn't want you to know."

Hurt grips my vocal cords, making my throat feel thick with pain.

I come to my feet in an instant, frustration oscillating inside of me like a wrecking ball. I'm trying really hard not to be mad. It's harder than I thought. "Yet you knew it was me—Mabel—all along. Otherwise, you wouldn't have called me Bel. Nobody but *you* calls me that."

Liam surges too and it really registers in my mind that it's *him*. Liam, who I've been dying to see for two years. Liam, who's been my pillar of strength for two years. Liam, who has evaded all my attempts at seeing him.

And when I look past the physical appearance, I realize that the way he's been acting towards me for the last half an hour—kind, protective, a bit shy—is very much *my* Liam. As well as his love for building things. Still, there's no way I could have recognized him considering he's never let me see a glimpse of him.

"How did you know I was Bel?" I whisper.

He shakes his head, having the decency to look ashamed. "I've always known how you looked, babe. You weren't hard to find online."

Essentially, he stalked my Instagram and never told me in any of our texts. Nice. I obviously wasn't hard to find since my bio contained a short description—20, Canadian Filipina model, marketing student—and Liam, as we established, knows me like the back of his hand.

He doesn't have social media—or at least, that's what he told me—so it's not like I could have ever returned the favour. Hell, I've gone through many Liam O'Connell accounts, but there's no way I could have known which one was his.

Betrayal burns like acid in my stomach.

"Yet you never gave me the courtesy of knowing how you looked."

My sharp words cause him to wince. Good. I want him to feel the hurt I'm feeling. It may be irrational, but I hate how hoodwinked I feel right now.

"Is this some kind of joke to you? You know how long I've been wanting to meet you, Liam, and I've done everything in my power to show you that you can trust me." The words are wrenched out of my chest and drip with anguish. "I was so upset when you canceled tonight, saying you couldn't make it. But here you are in the flesh. Shit, Liam, you *never* even told me you worked at MacGregor. Do you know how bad this looks?"

The time we shared just now feels cheap. I feel played and I wish I could make myself see past the red blurring my vision.

"Bel, please." Liam steps forward and his scent—pinewood and something utterly masculine—envelopes me. I can't think straight with him so close, clouding my thoughts. "I hate that I've upset you. This isn't how I wanted things to go."

"Then tell me what was going through your mind when you sat here and talked to me like I was a stranger to you," I grate. "Make me understand why you lied and introduced yourself as Lee instead of Liam."

Liam's hand reaches out. I don't grasp it back. Hurt, he drops it to his side. I loathe that I ache seeing this big, gorgeous man in pain because of me.

Anyone can walk by and see our showdown in the hallway. Suddenly, I'm feeling exposed and extremely uncomfortable. I hate confrontations. I just want to be transported back to my room in the safety of my bed with my cat.

"I knew you were coming tonight, but I wasn't ready for you to meet me, Bel," Liam says regretfully. My entire body jolts. "Then I saw you get hit and I couldn't stand to see you hurt on my watch. So I offered you some ice and...I wanted to be close to you. I'm aware I screwed up this whole situation, but I swear it wasn't my intention. Please believe me."

I'm still reeling from what he said before. "Why weren't you ready for me to meet you?"

"I can't explain it." His hand roves down his barrel chest and belly anxiously. "I'm sorry."

At the end of the day, I can't force Liam to speak his mind if he doesn't want to. It hurts like hell, and I give up.

"Yeah, well, it doesn't matter anymore," I retort, shaking my head. "Thanks for the surprise reveal, Liam."

His blue eyes go wide. "Bel—"

I'm already whirling around and marching down the hallway, heading straight for the bar. I need to call Kennedy and tell her that our forty minutes are over. I held up my end of the bargain.

I can't be here anymore.

Liam is still calling out to me. I hear his loud footsteps as he approaches. I pick up speed until I'm practically fast-walking slash jogging in my heels.

This isn't how I thought our first meeting would go.

The hurt in my chest spreads like wildfire through my body until I'm consumed by it. It's fueling my desire to run away from Liam and this so-called friendship of ours.

"Bel, wait, please!" he shouts.

I merge into the crowd of bar-goers and make my escape out the front door, my phone plastered to my ear as I call Kennedy.

Fresh air barely calms me down.

It feels like someone carved my insides with a knife and now I'm bleeding a bloody trail in my wake.

As I breathe laboured and tilt my head skyward, I come to the conclusion that Liam's actions hurt me beyond words because of my feelings for him.

I guess none of that matters anymore, though.

Because I'm done with Liam.

So fucking done.

CHAPTER 5

Liam

I have messed up on a colossal level.

There's no denying it.

It's been six days since Mabel ran out of MacGregor after our quarrel.

No wonder she left with a broken-hearted expression. She made herself vulnerable by telling me how badly she'd been wanting to see me and all I gave her was a "I wasn't ready for you to meet me, Bel." No other explanation. Just that. What an asshole thing to do.

It's also been six nights since Mabel started ignoring my text messages.

Never in my life have I felt this low.

The worst part is I deserve to feel this way.

I've spent the last few days self-reflecting on the situation and wishing I could have gone about the entire thing differently.

Driving a stake through my chest would have been less painful than seeing the desolate glint in her soft brown eyes as she ran away.

God, I put that look on her face. I made her sad. I'm not supposed to make her sad. I'm supposed to love and protect her. Always.

It's Thursday night and I'm working the closing shift with Pia. Well, she's working and I'm sulking, sitting on a stool by the bar with a non-alcoholic beer bottle cradled in my hands.

I stare at it like it holds the answers to all my questions.

News flash: it does not.

The bar is empty except for us two. Everyone else has gone

home. The sound of Pia counting the cash and the low drone of an RnB song ring in the background. But none of them are louder than the self-loathing simmering in my soul.

I pride myself on being a calm man. I'm level-headed and I go out of my way to keep my emotions at bay when I'm working. However, tonight was a huge test of my self-restraint. I broke up three drunken fights between a handful of frat boys and actually had to stop myself from throwing a punch to let out steam.

Everything and everyone is irritating me. I hate this purgatory I'm stuck in, a constant hell filled with nothing but my misery.

Since we first exchanged numbers a year ago, Mabel and I have never gone more than a day or two without texting. I don't know how to deal with this separation and it's taking a toll on me.

Even the people around me are beginning to notice it.

Especially Pia, who was quick to point out that my beard has seen better days and the bags under my eyes remind her of a Tim Burton character. Gotta love Pia. She knows how to kick a man when he's already down.

I take a swig of my beer and drop the bottle down with a louder *thunk* than necessary.

Pia rolls her eyes like I'm insufferable to deal with, then advances towards me in her pint-sized glory. "All right, grumpy. I'm sick and tired of seeing you brood. Let's have at it. Tell me what's bothering you."

"Nothing is bothering me," I grit out.

Pia cocks her hip against the counter and tsks. "Yeah, I don't believe you. I'm willing to bet all my tips tonight that it starts with *May* and ends with *Bel*."

Just the mention of her name sends a pang of longing through my chest. "Please, Pia. Drop it. I don't want to talk about it."

"No. We are talking about it. You can't isolate yourself whenever you're hurt. It's not healthy."

"You offering to play my therapist, P?"

"If that's what it takes to get you out of this mood, then yeah, call me Dr. Phil."

I want to tell her about all these thoughts jumbled in my brain. However, I'm not great at accepting help or discussing my feelings. More so when it's related to my love life (or lack of). Sure, Mabel and I have had plenty of deep conversations about life, but even with her, I felt...embarrassed relaying my past.

Or the way she makes me feel.

Chancing one more glance at Pia, I bite the bullet. "I screwed up with Bel."

"No shit, Sherlock. That much is obvious." She grimaces seeing the devastated look on my face. "Sorry, I didn't mean to be rude. Why don't you start at the beginning? Explain to me why you never told her who you were."

Downing the last bit of my beer, I move the bottle aside and Pia takes it away. My cheeks heat up (another thing I hate about myself: I blush easily) as I ponder how to best say it.

I finally rip the bandage. "I feel unworthy of her."

Pia gapes at me. "What?"

"C'mon, Pia. Everyone who sees us standing next to each other must wonder what a guy like me is doing with a girl like Mabel."

"Please, tell me this is a joke."

I wish it were.

When I remain silent, Pia's expression shifts to something horrified. "You truly think badly of yourself."

I can't even deny it. I always have. The curse of being bullied growing up? Every single bad thing someone has ever said about me is etched in my mind. Sometimes I can shake off those thoughts. Sometimes they consume me.

Those thoughts make me feel undeserving of having good things.

My self-esteem has taken a dive over the last few years and I've been doing my damnedest to bring it back up. Some days are a challenge, while others are a bit easier.

"Lee." Pia reaches forward and squeezes my closed fist. "I've met a lot of men in my twenty-seven years on this earth, and I can say with confidence that you're one of the most noble of them all. I've never seen you speak to anyone with disrespect, you treat everyone you meet with kindness, and you never let the female patrons walk alone at night to their cars. Not to mention, I've seen you defend girls when unwanted boys get a little too handsy with them. You're the kind of guy who restores my faith in mankind."

My throat tightens with emotions as I soak in Pia's genuine words.

"And these are just the things I've seen working with you for a short while. I have no doubt that the people who know you closely echo this sentiment: you're a fantastic human being. I don't know much about your past, but I'm very sorry to know it's made you see yourself in such a bland light."

My chest feels like it's squeezing. With pain. With happiness. With relief. I have a hard time accepting compliments because I so rarely get them. "You should really consider a career as a therapist, P."

She chuckles good-naturedly. "I'm an excellent listener and advice-giver, thank you. I'm well-aware of my talents."

I tug at the collar of my black polo self-consciously. "Do you think I deserve a girl like...Mabel?"

Pia gives me a soft smile. "I think you deserve each other, Lee. Mabel seems like a sweetheart and honestly? Any woman would be lucky to have a man like you. You're special and I believe she knows it too. The way she gazed at you Friday night, like she was completely enamoured, speaks volumes." Pia braces her elbows on the counter and leans forward, frowning. "Are you sure she's never told you how she feels about you? I have a hard time believing she hasn't dropped any hints."

I freeze for a moment, the last two sentences circling in my mind on a loop.

Pia watches me silently, her gaze burning into mine with intent.

Mabel was gazing at me like she was completely enamoured?

I do recall pieces from last Friday night where Mabel smiled at me in... wonderment. The way she had a hopeful twinkle in her eyes, despite feeling wretched, when she asked me if I was Liam. Before her disappointment at my fuckup, there was an instant when her face flashed with happiness.

Realization dawns upon me slowly at first and then escalates in a domino-like effect when I push aside my insecurities and really think about my relationship with Mabel.

My mind conjures up little snippets of our conversations. Mabel calling me the bestest best friend. Mabel telling me she adores me. Mabel declaring me as perfect, without having once seen me.

Oh, God.

She called you perfect and you hurt her. The only girl in the entire world who's shown you true happiness and you actually fucking hurt her.

This whole time, I think I'm the only one dealing with a bad case of unrequited love. Now I'm riddled with the possibility that Mabel may have felt something for me beyond the boundaries of a platonic friendship.

Fuck, fuck, fuck.

Has Mabel been trying to tell me in her own ways what she feels and

I've been too daft to hear it because of my own negativity? Goddammit, did I sabotage my own chances with her because I took too long to pull my head out of my ass?

Even worse…Have I ruined us forever?

No, no, no. Please, no. Anything except for that.

"Based on the face you're making, I gathered Mabel likes you and you took *wayyy* too long to realize it?" Pia winces when I rub a hand over my face in panic. She lays a comforting hand on my shoulder and gives it a little shake. "Take my advice, Lee, and reach out to her again. If she truly cares about you, she'll hear you out."

I nod, running my fingers through my hair. "You're right. I have to reach out to her."

Pia grins, trying to set me at ease. "Don't worry. Everything will be okay."

I'm so very thankful Pia and I had this conversation. Everything she said resonates and now I know what I need to do.

Anything and everything in my power to make amends.

I need Mabel to give me a *chance.*

Because God as my witness, I want to be with this girl. I want it more than I've ever wanted anything in my life. I may not feel deserving of her, but I'll make it my life's mission to be everything she wants and needs.

I love Mabel Garcia.

I have for two years.

Now it's time for me to finally show it to her.

I stand up from the stool and shrug on my flannel jacket. "Thank you, P, for everything. I needed to hear this."

Pia reaches forward to lightly punch my shoulder, her eyes shining with pride. "You're welcome. Now stop wasting time and go get your girl, Lee."

My girl.

For the first time in days, I breathe better. Hope wins the war of torment raging inside of me. I actually find I have a shot at winning back Mabel.

After closing, I walk Pia to her car and then hightail it to mine, my thumb moving over my phone screen as I press the call button. It may be 2:00 a.m., but Mabel is a night owl. There's a strong possibility she'll answer.

It rings once.

Twice.

Thrice.

I'm nervous. I've never called her before. I'm equal parts excited and worried about her picking up. There's no big speech I've rehearsed. Just my honest truth ready to go.

You're it for me, Bel. My forever girl. Give me one more chance to make this right. Please. I miss you. I love you.

On the fifth ring, it goes to voicemail.

Hearing her voice after days is like a balm to my bleeding wound.

"Hey, it's May. Sorry I can't come to the phone right now. Leave me a message after the beep."

Can't say I'm surprised she didn't pick up. She's still hurt and it's valid. She needs time, and I want to give her time…But not too much.

"Hey, Bel." My heart pounds fast. "It's Liam. I…I was hoping we could talk and you'd give me the opportunity to explain some things. I miss you and would love to hear from you soon, babe."

The words *I love you* are on the tip of my tongue.

But I want to see Mabel's face the first time I say them.

And I pray to God that my girl feels the same way about me.

CHAPTER 6

Mabel

It's been a hundred and sixty-eight hours since I spoke to Liam.

But who's keeping count, right?

The hurt I felt has now turned into a dull ache that pulsates every now and then as I go about my day-to-day life. School and social media have taken up a big chunk of my time.

I've kept myself busy to remain distracted.

That way I don't have to think about Liam.

Which is a difficult task considering every night when I lie in bed and close my eyes, the first thing I see is his blue gaze reminiscent of an ocean. My traitorous mind paints his shy smile, nestled into his brown beard. My fingers itch to run through it to see if it feels as soft as it looks. And my hands yearn to run over that tall, hefty body, just to see how his muscles bunch and shift under my touch.

God, I'm hopeless.

Even my mom and dad know something isn't status quo when I enter our home on the seventh day of Liam's and my separation—*if* you can even call it that.

I hear their low murmurs and follow the sound until I reach the threshold of the dining room. They're sitting at the table, playing checkers with the new set I gifted them last week.

I love my parents and I love providing for them. My dad is an electrician and my mom is a dental assistant and both have worked extremely hard their whole lives for my sake. One day when I've made good money from either my degree or modelling, I'm going to retire them early. So they can enjoy quiet moments like this one: playing board games at night with oldies tunes droning in the background.

My dad's face breaks into a wide smile when he spots me. The corners of his brown eyes—the ones I inherited—crinkle endearingly and he greets me. *"Kumusta anak ko?"*

My parents raised me to speak both my mother tongues—Tagalog and English—fluently.

"Mabuti po," I tell him I'm doing good and ask how he is, *"Kayo ho?"* Then I glance at my mother, who's watching us warmly. "Hi, Mom. How's it going?"

"Hi, sweetie." She places her hot cocoa on a coaster. My dad quickly makes his next move. "Good. How was your quiz today?"

I sigh, bone-deep. "Not so great. I'm just hoping I passed."

Unfortunately, I really screwed up on the last set of multiple-choice questions because I didn't study hard enough for one module.

"Oh, no." Her face falls and both my parents bestow me with matching frowns. "Sorry to hear that, May."

I shrug my purse off my shoulder and onto the crook of my elbow. "It's okay. I've been doing well in this class anyway and this quiz isn't worth a lot."

It's a mere three percent. I'll easily bounce back.

My dad adjusts his glasses and regards me with renewed encouragement. "Don't worry. You'll do better next time."

"Thank you." I go to give them each a forehead kiss. Something I've been doing since I was a little girl.

My mom grabs me before I can pull away and searches my face. "Is something else bothering you, Mabel? You've been very…quiet lately."

My mom's extremely observant. Nothing flies over her head. She always knows when something is wrong, picking up on the smallest telltale sign. It's no secret my demeanor has been off this entire week. And while I'm close to my parents, I just don't have it in me to rehash the whole Liam fiasco.

"Everything is fine," I reassure. She can tell I'm lying but doesn't push it. "I already had dinner after class, so I'm going to go to bed straight away."

My parents wish me good night with wavering smiles coated with worry.

In the shower, I cry a few tears. It happens all of a sudden. It's uncontrollable and I blame it on the fact that Aunt Flo will be visiting soon. Even though I'm in denial and fully aware that it has everything to do with my crappy week.

When I come out of the shower, completely shaved and moisturized in my favourite lemon-scented lotion, I notice a plate of *turon* sitting on my bed. Surprise, surprise, that makes me cry too. My dad always brings me treats when I'm feeling down. It's the fact that he *knew* and wordlessly brought up one of my favourite desserts to silently cheer me up.

Cheeto also has her suspicions that something isn't right once I settle into my bed after putting on a face mask and lighting up my cozy fall candles. I like to think animals are very much in tune with their humans' emotions. My cat has been staring at me with her judgemental (or is it concerned?) stare while I watch reruns of *The Vampire Diaries.*

"Elena, how could you?" I holler at my screen when Elena and Damon kiss. It's official. Season four sucks. "Stefan deserves so much better!"

The only person who would agree with me is Liam. He's team Stelena (yes, I forced him to binge-watch the show). But I'm not replying to any of his text messages, having ignored all of them for days.

My wound is still raw, even though I miss him like crazy.

After mulling over our last encounter, my self-reflection concludes the following: Liam not wanting to meet in person truly has nothing to do with me and everything to do with his own scars. I want to be there for him. I want to help him. Yet I can't, unless I know what I'm working with.

That means Liam needs to open up and tell me where his mind's at so I can meet him halfway.

He's sent me plenty of apology text messages but none of them close to the spectrum of *let-me-explain-things-Bel.* It's all *I'm-sorry-and-I-messed-up.* The *why* isn't there.

Liam has strong walls, but he's going to have to lower them himself if he wants us to fix this.

And if I'm being completely honest, I don't think our friendship will go back to the way it used to be. Not when he'd murmured to me, in that hungry, awe-laced tone, *"You're so…beautiful. I wanted to tell you when I first saw you. Took my breath away, Bel."*

I'm not crazy or imagining things. Liam feels something for me beyond platonic best friendship.

So do I.

It took me a really long time to admit it to myself; I want more with Liam.

There will never be someone who treats or understands me the way he does.

My pondering is cut short when my phone blares. It's Kennedy. I pause my episode and pick up her video call, settling deeper into my pillows.

We're both wearing face masks, as is our ritual on Friday nights. "Hi, Ken."

"Hi, May." Kennedy settles onto a couch with a bowl of popcorn in her lap. "Sorry I couldn't call you earlier. I finished work late. A group of teenyboppers collectively spilled milkshakes all over the floor, so I was on mop duty."

"Ah, that sucks." I'd probably start wailing on my shift if that happened. "How are you feeling?"

"Tired and like I need to sleep for the next decade. I wanted to give you a call to catch up before I continued watching my boyfriend."

She's talking about Michael Cordero from *Jane the Virgin*. Not Caleb Wright, of course. We spoke about him a few days ago and Kennedy said she's over men and their mixed signals. She's laying off of them for a while and I don't blame her.

The only men we can rely on are of the fictional variety and written by women.

"Sounds like a perfect night." Cheeto stretches out and comes to rest on top of me. She likes to listen to my heartbeat sometimes.

Kennedy shoves another round of popcorn in her mouth. "Now tell me how *you're* doing. I know these last few days have been really stressful for you."

I deliberately avoid the elephant in the room: My unsuccessful romantic life. "My quiz went horribly."

"I'm sorry to hear that, May. On the bright side, you've been acing this class, so hopefully, it doesn't impact your final grade too much." Kennedy peels off her mask and hits me with a meaningful look that makes my stomach flip. "But you know that's not what I was referring to."

I sigh and peel off my own sheet mask. "Yeah. I know."

"Has he continued texting?"

"Every day." My chest twists at the painful reminder. "I'm so conflicted, Ken."

My best friend's face softens. "Mabel..."

"One part of me is mad at him, and the other part of me just wants to forgive and move on. I haven't ever gone this long without talking to Liam and I miss him so much."

"I know, but maybe you just need to give him the chance to speak to you once more and explain things—and not through texts. Some conversations

60

need to be had in person."

Everything Kennedy is saying makes sense.

I'll be the first one to admit I can be a little bit stubborn. It's probably why I haven't replied to Liam yet.

"You should answer him. Put yourselves out of your misery," Kennedy says. "The truth is you both don't want to be without each other, so you need to work this out. And even though you'll deny it, I know exactly how you feel about him."

My lips pinch together and I swallow with difficulty.

Kennedy gives me a pointed look.

The four-letter word.

I do feel it for Liam.

I have for a long time, if I'm being transparent.

How could I not have fallen for my shy, sweet, kind best friend who tends to all my needs, acts like my protector, and cherishes me wholly?

"I think he's it for me, Ken." I exhale slowly. "I want to…be with him."

Admitting it out loud is the best feeling I've had all week.

"Then be with him, May. He's given you an olive branch. It's time for you to reach out and grab it."

Kennedy is right. Liam knows he's made a mistake and he's been wanting to fix it.

It's time I heard him out.

After days of being stuck in limbo, my heart weighs lighter.

I thank Kennedy for being an amazing friend slash therapist slash personal hype-woman and we hang up.

Pulling up Liam's conversation, my thumb hovers over the screen as I read the last few text messages.

I'm sorry. I'm so fucking sorry, babe. —Liam

I know I've hurt you. It's the worst thing I've ever done in my life. —Liam

I messed up and I don't know how to make this right. Will you ever forgive me? —Liam

I can't stand this rift between us. I miss you so much, Bel. Miss your texts. Miss our banter. Miss it all. —Liam

Please, sunshine. Tell me how I can make things right again. —Liam

Bel, I'm begging you. Please don't think badly of me. I can stand it from others, but not from you. —Liam

I can't stop thinking about you. Day and night. You live in my mind. You have, since the first letter. —Liam

God, the way you looked that night, Bel... Didn't know a woman could be so perfect. —Liam

Don't even get me started on your voice. It's the loveliest thing I've ever heard. Soft. Raspy. Better than anything I've ever dreamed of. And I have dreamed of you. So often. You have no idea. —Liam

It pains me to know I might not ever hear it again. That you might never give me a chance to make things right. —Liam

That's the last text message.

However, I realize Liam called me late last night, but I missed it.

He left a voicemail.

I hold my breath and play it.

Then I listen to it again, and again, and again.

"Hey, Bel. It's Liam. I...I was hoping we could talk and you'd give me the opportunity to explain some things. I miss you and would love to hear from you soon, babe."

His deep voice, laced with yearning and sadness, tugs at my heartstrings.

The layer of ice covering my heart slowly starts to thaw. Finally, I see the silver lining. No matter what's been said and done, there is hope for Liam and me.

He's ready to explain things and now it's my turn to meet him halfway.

CHAPTER 7

Mabel

Saturday late afternoon, I finish wrapping up another successful lingerie photoshoot with a group of models. Every time I step into the studio, I'm gripped with a wave of gratitude and excitement that I get to do something I love with a team of talented individuals.

The girls want to go out for drinks at *La Flamme*, but I already made plans with Kennedy last night for a nice meal and movie.

Speaking of my best friend, she's supposed to come pick me up soon.

When I change into my royal blue minidress and strappy white heels, I power on my phone and see a missed message from Kennedy.

> May, I hate to do this, but I have to cancel. My grandma is feeling sick so I'm driving to her place with my mom. Can we reschedule? I'm so, so sorry. —Ken

I send back a text as I grab my bag and usher out of the studio.

> Nothing to apologize for, Ken! Send my love to your grandma. I hope she's doing okay <3 Give me an update when you can. xo —May

Unfortunately, I don't have my car with me since Kennedy was my ride. I can't call my parents either, since they've booked a romantic getaway at a spa on the outskirts of the city.

Technically, I can call an Uber.

When I step out into the busy downtown street, an odd sense

of loneliness grapples my insides. A result of being alone on a gorgeous fall afternoon. I wrap my trench coat around my frame tighter like a shield. Close by, a musician strums an Ed Sheeran song that spikes my nostalgia. Seeing the bustling faces of passersby as they go about their lives makes me feel out of place.

I stand against a brick wall, fixed in a moving crowd.

Ironically enough, my disposition mirrors my inner turmoil.

All I want at this moment is a sense of comfort.

There's only one person who can give that to me.

Only person I want with me, right here, right now.

Before I can convince myself otherwise, I text Liam. I hadn't replied to him last night because I wanted a clear head to focus on my work today. Now the cobwebs clouding my mind have dispersed and it's clear I've let this separation stretch between us for longer than necessary.

Hey, Liam…I need a big favour. —Bel

Anything. —Liam

He responds swiftly. Like he's been waiting all day for me to come to my senses.

I just finished a photoshoot and I need a ride. Will you come get me? —Bel

He doesn't reply for a solid minute.

Have I shocked him?

Oh, God. Maybe he's unavailable. Embarrassment heats my cheeks. It's Saturday, meaning he might be working at MacGregor. I should have thought about that before texting him.

Or I can just call an Uber. It's totally okay! —Bel

Don't call an Uber. I'll be there. Just text me the address. —Liam

My heart drums a fast beat. I text him my location.

It'll take me six minutes to get to you. —Liam

Oh, wow. I guess he was in the area.

I really appreciate it. Can we talk on the drive? —Bel

I'd love that. —Liam

A waiting game ensues and the anxious knot in my stomach gently unravels. I get so caught up in the musician singing his song that I startle when a hesitant, "Bel?" rings out behind me after a few minutes.

Pivoting around, I find Liam standing on the sidewalk next to a parallel parked SUV.

My warrior in shining armour's eyes are running over my body desperately, as though I'm a sight for his sore eyes. The way his lips part and a gentle sigh escapes him when I take a step his way nearly undoes me.

Liam O'Connell is magnificent to behold. More so when he stands there waiting for me with his heart on his sleeve. His gaze tells me what his words cannot. *You mean everything to me*, he's saying, *and I need you as badly as you need me.*

I cross the distance towards him. The crowd parts around us as we stand before one another. The sensation of home sinks into my bones.

"You came," I whisper.

Liam's blue gaze is alight with emotion. "You texted."

"Thank you, Liam." My hand reaches out for his.

He bridges the gap like he's been longing for me to hold his hand forever. "I'll always come for you, Bel. In a heartbeat. Night or day. No matter the time. That's my promise to you."

God, I love him.

Liam lifts my hand to his lips hesitantly and places a delicate peck. "You look incredible."

I turn to mush at his compliment.

My free hand skims down his robust torso. Tonight, he's wearing a grey sweater polo, black slacks, and polished brown shoes. The sleeves of his shirt are rolled up to his elbows, so I see his tattooed forearms and the silver watch circling his right wrist. My grumpy mountain man is so put together tonight and I'm practically drooling at the sight he creates. "You too look incredibly handsome."

Liam seems like he's about to pass out from my praise.

Before that can happen, he directs us towards the passenger side of his black SUV. He opens the door and I freeze when I notice a thick bouquet of sunflowers resting on the seat.

I arch my eyebrow.

Liam fumbles and his cheeks pinken as he hands me the bouquet. "I-I got these for you."

"When?" Because I can't fathom how this man was able to run the errand between now and my texts.

"Today, from your favourite florist." He glances away shyly. "I was going to call you again and see if you'd be willing to hear me out. If you said yes, I wanted to be prepared."

My heart is beating madly at his confession.

Leaning on my toes to kiss his bearded jaw is the only possible course of action.

So I do.

Liam's eyes widen. I actually feel the shiver that runs through his body. He's helpless to hide the effect I have on him.

"That was very sweet of you." My voice is hoarse. "Sunflowers are my favourites."

"I know," he says vehemently. "I know a lot of things about you, Bel, including all the things that make you happy. Those are the most important ones to me."

There's a lump the size of Canada lodged in my throat. "Because you want to make me happy?"

"I *only* ever want to make you happy. Though sometimes…I might screw up along the way." Liam squeezes the hand he's still holding. "I just need you to know that I'm far from perfect, but I want to be. For you."

I drop his hand and grasp his cheek in understanding.

Liam leans into my touch, his deep exhale hitting my wrist. "I'm sorry. Forgive me. Please."

For hurting me because those weren't his intentions. I get it now. I've had time to muse over our encounter and I'm ready to hear his side.

"Take me away, Liam." I brush his jaw lovingly. "Somewhere we can talk and put these last few days behind us."

CHAPTER 8

Mabel

Liam's car is all smooth leather, pine-scented haven.

He's cruising down the street, his fingers drumming against the steering wheel. The playlist running in the background is a medley of all our favourite tunes. I adore that Liam paid attention whenever I recommended songs. The fact that he listens to them as he drives is the cherry on top of the cake.

"Where are we going?" I adjust the bouquet in my lap.

I've caught Liam's eyes straying down to my bare thighs a handful of times. It's a wonderful stroke to my ego. Especially when his nostrils flare and he utters a prayer under his breath.

It's no secret that I'm attracted to my best friend.

I love that he's attracted to me too.

"I want to take you to my favourite spot. I like to go there whenever I need fresh air or just a moment of peace. You'll love it."

The moonroof is open and a gentle breeze grazes over our heads. A few pieces of my blowout float in the air. My view of Liam is partially obscured until I tuck my hair aside and lean my head against the leather headrest. There's something magical about the sun setting as we chase the night. Or maybe it has everything to do with the man sitting next to me. But I'm suddenly feeling flirty. The energy that crackled between us the first night we met pulsates again and I slither my hand so it rests on his strong thigh.

Liam's face turns just enough for our eyes to meet for a split second.

71

But the flash of hunger I see there fuels mine.

"Feed me first, Liam," I say saucily. "I'm starving."

Taking one hand off the steering wheel, he grabs my hand from his thigh and brings it to his mouth for another kiss. "What are you in the mood for?"

A celebratory meal. Some healthy communication. Then maybe a side helping of foreplay. In that particular order, of course.

"I could go for some chicken nuggets. And fries." I snap my fingers. "Oh, and an Oreo Mcflurry."

"Your wish is my command." He takes another left, redirecting us back to the East Side. "I could also go for a Mcflurry."

"Skor?"

He smiles bashfully. I know him so well. "Always."

I love this. How natural it feels to be in each other's presence. There's no awkwardness. The last few days of hurt just blur away. They're no longer prominent to me. Except for this moment.

Using my free hand, I run it over his jaw. "I really like your beard, Liam."

As I predicted, it's soft and well-maintained.

"Thank you," he says. "I've been using the beard oil you found for me all those months ago."

Another thing I adore about Liam? He's a skincare enthusiast like me and anything I suggest, he always tries out.

I stifle a laugh, picturing this big man sitting in front of his laptop, adding products to his Sephora cart because I asked him to.

"Do you still use the moisturizer I recommended?"

Liam drives with one hand, never letting go of mine. I find that so hot. "I use it every day, babe."

Damn, what is it about a grown-ass man who takes care of himself—and I'm talking hygiene, dressing nice, smelling divine—that just does it for me?

"How was work?" he asks.

"Exhausting, but good. I made friends with two new fellow models, who I'll probably run into during our next gig." I twirl the ends of my hair. "How was your day?"

"I finished building a birdhouse for our next door neighbour Mrs. Clifford. She's gotten a few visits from cardinals and blue jays in her backyard and she wants to be prepared for next summer." Liam grins, shaking his head. "She asked me to paint it pastel pink and add little red flowers."

My heart melts picturing Liam with a tiny paintbrush in his hands, adding little red flowers to a birdhouse in utmost concentration. "That's so cute. Does Mrs. Clifford still bake you madeleines every Sunday?"

"Yup." He chuckles. "I'm basically her surrogate grandson."

I chuckle too and then serenity floats in our space as we enjoy the beginning of a long evening.

I keep stealing glances at Liam.

Liam keeps stealing glances at me.

Where our words lack, our eyes speak in loud volumes.

I'm so happy you're here, I say.

There's nowhere else I'd rather be, he tells me.

We enter the driveway of McDonald's and my taste buds sigh in happiness. I can practically smell the greasy fries and taste the softness of the ice cream on my tongue.

I get ready to ask Liam a question, but it dies the second I catch him staring.

There's something dark and sensual in that gaze as it sweeps over me from head to toe. "I really like your dress, Bel."

Translation: I want to rip it off your body tonight.

And if he keeps looking at me like that, I'm going to turn feral and demand he take me into his back seat so we can do just that.

I cross my legs and he groans.

With a wink, I say flirtatiously, "I know."

After grabbing our food, Liam drives us to his spot.

It's absolutely perfect. The air is fresh, the sun is dipping low, and the water is glimmering like a cluster of crystals. The park is relatively empty except for a few locals who are feeding the ducks and an old couple taking a stroll.

Liam and I walk towards a wooden bench facing the water and sunset. We sit down and dig into our food with gusto.

I can feel Liam's grin when I finish my chicken nuggets and fries in Guinness record speed and then grab my Oreo McFlurry.

"You're an animal," he says with amusement, eating his own treat with the mannerism of a prince.

I put a spoonful of ice cream into my mouth and moan. "Mm, I could eat this for the rest of my life."

Liam's watching my lips with the same hunger that's usually reserved for a three-course meal at an expensive restaurant.

I smile devilishly around my spoon, licking it extra good for him. Just a little peep show—teaser really—for later, if he behaves. "Like what you see?"

"You have no idea."

My heart does a little somersault in its cage.

We continue eating our ice creams while enjoying the scenery around us. I can see why Liam likes coming here. It's calm, secluded, and resembles a sanctuary.

"Thank you for agreeing to talk," Liam finally begins. "These last few days…"

"Have sucked," I finish for him. "I didn't like the distance between us. Hated it. Not being able to message you every day. It made me feel restless and…"

"Like you were missing a part of you?" he asks hopefully.

I nod, staring at my feet.

Liam shifts on the bench, sliding just a teeny bit closer. He takes our garbage and dumps it into the McDonald's paper bag. I sense he needs a moment to collect his thoughts before speaking.

Eventually, he angles his face my way and I'm struck by the way his blue eyes glimmer in the late afternoon sky. "When I received your first letter in high school, you changed my life."

My lips part on a sharp inhale.

"For as long as I can remember, I've liked to hide behind my walls." He cracks his knuckles. "The world hasn't always been kind to me, therefore shielding myself was the only way I knew to live. If I was out of sight, I was out of mind, and nobody could hurt me. But that's not always the case, is it?"

I shake my head, needing him to elaborate. "Liam…"

"I was bullied growing up." His jaw clenches. "Unfortunately, my size has made me the target of many mean jokes. I was taller…*bigger*…than everyone and quieter by nature, which meant I struggled to make friends. As a result, it made me an outcast. Either people were avoiding me or if they spoke to me, it was usually to poke fun at my appearance. I can't begin to tell you how I survived high school. But if there's one way to sum up my experience, it's the word *shitty*. The way people treated me only pushed me deeper into my solitude. I had one close friend, who'd also been dubbed a loser by the popular kids, so he and I stuck together. Eventually, he moved away and I was back to being alone."

I'm holding my breath when Liam glances my way again. One part of me is content he's opening up, but another part is in pain hearing this out loud.

It was obvious Liam had somewhat of a difficult past.

I just didn't know he was *bullied*.

Protectiveness surges in me like a tsunami. The need to go back in time and kick the asses of all the jerks who hurt Liam is so strong, I can barely articulate it.

"Are you okay?" Liam asks, staring at the white quality of my knuckles.

"No, I'm not." I let out a humourless chuckle. "But I need you to continue with your story before I lose my shit and demand names and addresses. So I can do bodily harm, of course."

Liam unwinds my closed fists and weaves our fingers together. He brings them to his mouth for a kiss. I've lost track of how many times he's done that today. It grounds me, though. Maybe it grounds him too. "Be at ease, Bel. I'm fine now. That was the past and although it can't be changed, I only want to move forward now."

I can't speak, so I only nod.

Liam continues talking, but he never lets my hands go. His thumb caresses my wrist, as though telling my pulse to *steady*. "As I was saying, high school was a shitshow. I did everything in my power to be invisible so people would leave me alone. Then came the start of senior year and I met this girl. She actually found me one day in the school library, sitting in my corner reading a fantasy novel during lunchtime." Liam squeezes my hands. "Turns out she wanted to read it too. We struck a camaraderie and eventually, she started coming to the library every day to...hang with me. She liked my company, but she didn't want people to know we were friends. I guess it would put a target on her back, considering she was part of the popular crew. And as I mentioned before, I wasn't."

I hate where this is going. My stomach drops even before Liam says the next bit.

He takes a deep inhale and closes his eyes. "She was nice to me and naturally, I started liking her. I never dared to ask her out because I was scared of rejection. Plus, I wasn't certain how she felt about me. Despite her friendliness, on most days, I just felt like her dirty secret." Liam caresses my knuckles absentmindedly. "I didn't know it at the time, but she had a boyfriend on the basketball team. He was one of the popular jocks. He found us one day and all hell broke loose. She told him we were just friends and the only reason she hung out with me was out of pity." Liam puffs out a self-deprecation laugh. "Safe to say he got mad and then…him and his buddies beat me up after school."

My eyes water, tears threatening to spill. "*No*."

Liam sighs, nodding. "Yes. They beat me up badly. It was four against one and I couldn't defend myself. After a few minutes, I gave up and just let it happen. I was numb. I just wanted it over with so I could crawl back home and be in the comfort of my bed to sleep off that nightmare. I only screamed when one of the guys pulled out his pocket knife and dug it into my cheek. That's where this comes from." He brings my trembling hand to the scar on his cheek. It's thin, white, and almost masked by his beard. "Eventually, a janitor heard the commotion and came to my rescue." Liam exhales slowly. "By then, I had a swollen jaw, bruised eye, sore ribs, and a bleeding cheek."

A tear escapes my eye.

It's like someone ripped out my heart and stomped on it.

I'm afraid if I open my mouth, I'll start sobbing and Liam won't continue telling his story.

"The part that hurts the most? The girl knew they were going to beat me up after school and she didn't bother giving me a heads-up. If she had, I would have skipped the next period and hauled my ass home as soon as possible."

"Names. Addresses," I spit through gritted teeth. "I'm going to kill her. And the boys who did that to you."

My words incite a boyish smile to curl Liam's lips. Ever so gently, he leans forward to brush his lips over my tear. Kissing it away. Like I'm the one who needs comfort.

Despite what he's been through, he's so soft and gentle and that only makes me cry harder.

"You mean more to me than I can ever put into words, *mo chrot*." Liam kisses both my cheeks, removing all traces of the tears I'm crying for him. "You make my world a better place. I beg you. Please, don't cry. It hurts me to see you sad."

Doesn't he get it?

It hurts *me* to know he was treated this way. That I can do nothing but sit here passively while he relays the saddest thing I've ever heard. That I can't teach his bullies the lesson they deserve.

Because no one is allowed to touch my Liam in violence. Ever.

I want to protect him from all the harm in the world. I want to show him love, kindness, and laughter. I want to give him good memories that'll overshadow anything bad he's ever experienced.

I want to tell Liam that he'll never be alone—that he'll always have me from this day forward. And that I will always safeguard him to the best of my ability, in the cradle of my arms, in the warmth of my soul, in the protective cage of my heart.

But that can wait until he's done speaking his side.

"Please tell me what happened afterwards, Liam," I plead, praying there's something positive on the other side of this ugly story.

"I went home and my parents saw my wounds. They went absolutely ballistic. The next day, they went to my school and threw a fit in the principal's office. The boys who beat me up were kicked off the basketball team and expelled once the janitor spoke in my defense. The faculty apologized many times, but the damage was already done." Liam's eyes tell me he's in memory lane. I despise that he's reliving this horror. "It took me a week to recover from that incident. The following Monday when I went back to school for the first time, I told myself I was going to ask my parents for homeschooling options. I didn't see the point in learning in an environment that failed to protect me. But then English class came around and my teacher distributed the first set of letters and…I got yours." Liam's thumb roved over my cheek in reverence. "And it brought me solace in a time where I felt desolate. You represented hope to me, Bel. You always have and you always will."

Overwhelmed by my feelings for this guy, I bring our joined hands to my mouth for a kiss. My lips meet the tattooed IV on his thumb.

No matter what happens now, he and I are in it for the long run.

"You were like a ray of sunshine entering my life after many dark days. I had the biggest smile on my face when I was reading your letter. You were so chatty and telling me all these things about yourself." There's a fond twinkle in his eyes. "And then you demanded to know everything about me.

For the first time in my life, someone my age was taking a genuine interest in me. It was surprising, but so very welcomed. You made me feel seen and heard. It was only a matter of weeks before you became my best friend. Before I...fell for you."

He fell for me.

Same as I fell for him.

"Oh, Liam." My smile and voice are shaky. "Writing to you was my solace too. I could feel your selflessness and your big heart in every one of those letters. I loved learning everything about you. You fascinated me with your wisdom and your love for gardening and building things. I even looked forward to all the quotes you shared from your recent reads. Let's not forget how *you* also made me feel seen and heard. Especially after I told you what happened to me at the party two years ago and how it messed with my mind. You were always there for me, Liam. I too fell for you within a matter of weeks."

There's a wild look in his eyes as I confess my feelings.

But before we can move forward with this—*us*—there's one more urgent thing to discuss. "Liam, I need to know why you weren't ready to meet me. Please. It's been bothering me since you mentioned it. I've been dying to see you for two years. I could feel you wanting the same, but you always pulled back. Why?"

Silence falls around us.

The waves and the chirping birds fill the empty space.

I never look away from my best friend.

Liam inhales and takes my palm, placing it on his bearded jaw. "Take a good look at me, Bel." He smiles wryly. "I'm not the prettiest boy on the block."

Shock robs me of breath.

"The first time I saw your picture, I stopped breathing. I'd never seen someone so gorgeous. Every inch of you, babe. Pure fucking perfection." He swallows hard. "You're my dream girl, Bel, and I look like a monster in comparison to you."

"Are you fucking kidding me right now?"

He looks absolutely serious.

I almost start wailing, my heart twisting painfully for this foolish man who can't even see his own beauty. "Liam, you're not monster-looking. Nor are you pretty. That word doesn't do you justice." I shake my head. "You're absolutely *stunning*. Inside and out. I nearly orgasmed the first time I saw you at the bar."

"Fuck." His expression softens. "Are you serious?"

"Cross my heart and hope to die." I spent so much of my time empowering others through my platform; I hate that my own best friend was here, on the other side, feeling so horrible about himself. I don't care what anyone else has to say. This man is a complete ten in my book. He's so sexy and I wish he could see himself from my point of view. "The next time you look in the mirror, I want you to see what I see, Liam."

"What do you see?" he hushes with a vulnerable edge.

"I see my present and my future. I see my best friend." I frame his face with my hands and gaze into his eyes. "I see *my* Liam, the man of my dreams."

Liam exhales roughly, releasing days' worth of tension. His forehead drops to mine, his baby blues finally seeing my truth. "You're everything to me," he murmurs. "I've wanted to kiss you for two years now. Can I, Bel?"

"Yes." I begin to erase the distance between our lips. "Kiss me, Liam."

Liam's hands cup my face and he meets me halfway, stamping his mouth to mine with a low groan.

Yearning and potent passion drive the kiss, which begins butterfly-soft and turns into something raring as we become restless for one another. Our mouths brush and sip impatiently like we just can't get enough, just can't get closer, just can't wait to be one. The need to descend into his skin and build a forever home inside him is jarring.

My hands trickle down to his collar. I pull him impossibly closer. Liam's soft beard tickles my chin and I moan when his tongue darts across the seam of my lips, asking for permission.

He has it.

Our tongues meet, savouring the sweet taste of this new love.

Liam's hands grow in confidence, palming my hips. In one swift jerk, he yanks me over his lap. God, the strength of this man. I break the kiss with a gasp and feel Liam's answering, almost cocky, smirk.

Then he's back to stealing my air until I no longer remember where he begins and where I end.

My mind runs on an endless loop of *Liam, Liam, Liam*.

His hands are in my hair. On my body. Over my curves. He kneads my ass and thighs with a masculine grunt, like he can't get over how amazing I am. I'm doing the same. Exploring his shoulders. His barrel chest. His thick middle. And then returning to his luscious hair so I can angle his head back and kiss him deeper.

There's nothing sweet about the kiss anymore.

It's savage, needy, and hot.

Liam O'Connell doesn't kiss like a gentleman.

I'm hoping he doesn't fuck like one either.

We break apart with lustful noises. Liam's breath puffs against my parted mouth, his eyes half-mast and glazed. My warrior looks conquered after one kiss and I'm addicted to the look on his face, a mixture of torment and wonder. The golden glow of the setting sun really gives him the allure of a battle-hardened warrior coming home to his true love.

Me being the true love, of course.

"That was perfect," I huff, grinning as I attempt to tame his hair after messing it.

Liam snags my lips in another quick kiss. "*You* are perfect."

There I go again, falling even deeper for him.

"Right back at you." I press my forehead to his while staring into his eyes. "Every inch of you. Pure fucking perfection, babe."

I throw the words back at him and his answering grin lights up my entire being.

Liam, whilst taking my compliment, is still struggling with it. I'm no fool; I'm well aware that the bullying he's experienced has taken a toll on him. I swear I'll spend every single day reminding him how perfect he is until we get past this.

"You're the guy for me, Liam," I vow. "My world is a better place because you exist in it too. Never forget that."

My statement is worming its way into his core. It's evident in the way his hands tighten on my waist and the way his eyes gleam. I understand exactly what he wants to say, without him having to voice it aloud.

"God, Bel. Nobody makes me feel the way you do."

Smiling, I fuse my mouth to his and then there's no more talking. Just feeling one another. Our kisses go from PG-13 to downright X-rated when I feel his bulge.

I grind against it experimentally.

"This is public indecency," Liam groans, fingers digging into my thighs like he doesn't want me to stop.

"Yeah, well, I don't see any cops trying to stop us," I say playfully, sucking on his bottom lip and tugging.

"Bel," Liam growls under his breath and the sound sets my thong on fire. As if I wasn't already wet. "You're killing me."

I place tiny kisses on his jaw until I reach his ear. "We should take this somewhere more private…like in the back seat of your car."

CHAPTER 9

Liam

"**W**e should take this somewhere more private...like in the back seat of your car."

Those words ricochet inside my skull and pierce the thin veil of my self-restraint. When I received the text from Bel earlier today, I thought we'd simply talk and fix things.

Never in a million years did I expect the love of my life to kiss me, much less grind on my lap like I'm her personal pleasure toy. Fuck, I love this girl. I love her so much I'm bursting at the seams with it.

Now she wants me to take her to the back seat of my car.

Is this what it feels like to win the lottery?

"As you wish, sunshine." Grabbing Mabel, I throw her over my shoulder fireman style.

She squeals and laughs throatily at the unexpected move. I grin. My best friend hasn't said it outright, but she enjoys my strength and how easily I can overpower her.

I reckon she'll love being bossed and tossed around in bed.

Damn, I'm already thinking of a homerun when I've barely passed second base with her. My mind has stored many fantasies over the course of two years. I've imagined the raunchiest scenarios while jacking off, my phone clenched in my hand as I stare at Bel's thirst traps.

My fast strides carry us towards the parking lot, where my car is parked in a secluded spot overshadowed by a canopy of tree branches. Mabel giggles at my haste and I swear that sound causes my heart to thrum like the strings of an acoustic guitar.

"Someone is impatient," she jests.

"I've been wanting you for two years, Bel. Impatient isn't the word I'd use."

"Yeah?" she challenges when I open the back seat door of my SUV and shove her inside. "What would you use?"

I climb after her and close the door, locking us in. "*Aching*. Like I'll die if I stop touching you."

When our eyes collide, words suddenly fail me.

I'll never forget the sight of Mabel's tall, curvy body draped against the leather seat, cast in half shadows and half warm glow from the setting sun. Her hair is a tumbled mess from my restless hands. Her eyes weighed down with desire. Her bottom lip playfully caught between her pearly white teeth.

Mabel Garcia is a divine being.

A nymph straight out of a fantasy novel, oozing sensuality and invoking erotic urges.

There is no doubt that her beauty is coveted by thousands of people, but it's her sassy attitude and nurturing soul that have had me in a chokehold from the start.

I want to treat Mabel like a queen and kiss the very ground she walks on. I whisper a prayer to the universe to give me the opportunity to show this incredible girl the world, for she deserves nothing less.

Mabel smiles wickedly and widens her legs, the invitation clear as day. "Then come touch me, Liam."

I pounce on her.

Hauling her into my lap, I settle comfortably against the seat and attack her neck with gentle love bites and teeth nips. Her shriek melts into a languid chuckle.

"You like being manhandled, sweetheart?"

"Only by you."

"What else do you like?" I'm ravenous for her. I redirect her lips to mine for a kiss.

It's nasty, sloppy, and gets me hotter than ever.

Bel can feel my hardening cock. She sits firmly atop my crotch and grinds in slow, torturous movements meant to drive me completely insane. "I like the feel of your hands on my body. I like the way you wrap your arms around me and make me feel safe. I like—no, *love*—the taste of your lips. I've thought about kissing you incessantly for two years. Some nights, the thought has kept me awake until I…"

I groan, my fingers digging into her waist. "Until you what?"

I'm holding my breath, hoping Mabel will say what I think she'll say.

"Until my fingers find their way into my panties and I'm touching myself."

I almost pass out hearing her filthy confession.

Not too long ago, I wouldn't believe a girl like her could want a guy like me. But after airing out our feelings, I understand Mabel's been a goner for me since the beginning.

The same way I've been a goner for her.

"You touch yourself often to the thought of me?" It's almost too good to be true.

"At least once a week." She mewls when I tug her bottom lip with my teeth, her fingers denting my brawny shoulders. "I usually lie in bed, going over our conversations and fucking myself until I come all over my hand. You drive me crazy whenever you call me *babe* or praise me for the smallest things."

Lust sledgehammers inside my core, imagining this girl playing with her wet pussy. Because I got her all hot and bothered with my words. Because I'm the guy of her dreams.

All because of *me*.

"I used to envision what you'd look like, Liam." Mabel's finger traces my lips in adoration. "However, the reality of you blows away anything I've ever imagined. I don't think a word exists in the English language to describe your handsomeness, but if I had to settle for one thing, I'd say you resemble a real-life warrior. One that's all mine to keep forever."

Anything I could have said in return dies in my throat.

This girl.

This fucking perfect girl.

"I must have done something right in my past life to deserve you." I clutch the nape of her neck and draw her forehead to mine. "There's no one like you. There will never be someone like you for me. You're it. You're in my veins, in my blood, in my goddamned bruised heart. You're everywhere and when I close my eyes, all I feel and see is you, Mabel."

A strangled noise escapes her and Mabel presses her mouth to mine in a violent kiss. It's the kind of kiss where we know there's no going back. We're headed straight for the final happily-ever-after in our fairy tale.

I will make all her wishes come true, I swear to myself, as I lose myself in her rousing kisses and the smell of her—sunshine and lemons.

"Bel," I groan like an animal as she lays hungry kisses all over my neck like she's addicted and can't get enough. "Will you let me please that pretty pussy of yours, baby?"

I'm surprised I said it out loud, but honesty is the best policy.

She stops and raises her head, panting, "Y-You want to?"

"I've been fantasizing about it forever."

Mabel's mouth quirks up. Her lipstick is smudged. I love seeing her dolled up. But I also like seeing her dishevelled because of my touch. "What else have you been fantasizing about?"

I lick my lips, catching the remnant of her taste, and say, "You sitting on my face and soaking my beard like a naughty little bad girl."

Mabel blinks a few times.

Her mouth opens and closes, but no sentences come out.

I think I've sent the poor girl into shock.

I rub her waist to bring her back to earth. "You okay, babe?"

She blushes and finally lets out a long exhale. "Oh, wow. Um, yeah. That…that sounds great, Liam. I'd love to sit on your face. Really. I'm game."

I chuckle and kiss her jaw. "You like it when I talk dirty?"

She nods earnestly.

"Good. I've got more where that came from."

"Tell me, Liam."

"I want to put you on your hands and knees and spread you wide-open for my cock," I murmur in her ear, relishing the way the lines in her body tighten at my words. "I want to watch you whine and moan and claw at the sheets as you take every inch of me." My fingers draw down her back until I'm clutching her hips. "And I want to fuck you so hard, you never forget what it's like to be owned by me."

Mabel releases a low whimper.

My thumb grazes over her lips and when she parts them, I slip it inside, nearly coming in my pants when she sucks on the **IV** tattoo with the coyest expression on her features.

With my other hand, I push the short hem of her dress higher up her thighs, caressing one of her dimples. "Every time you posted a shot wearing a sundress or a filthy little swimsuit, were you hoping I'd chance upon it?"

"Y-Yes. Some part of me wanted you to find me and be…"

"Tempted?" I supply. "Obsessed?" I squeeze her inner thigh. "Because one look at you and I was fucking ruined, Bel. I've taken screenshots of every single one of your pictures. I look at them every night when I wrap my fist around my cock and fuck myself in your honour."

"Liam." Her breathing goes a little harsh. "That was so bad of you."

"I know," I whisper, kissing her again. "Are you going to punish me for it?"

"I should," she pants, widening her stance until her knees are digging on either side of the seat and her pussy is practically glued over my bulge. "God, I *really* should."

"You've been secretly teasing me for two years now. Writing me all those sweet things in your messages. Telling me I'm the best thing to ever happen to you. Being a flirtatious little tease by sending me pictures of the nails I paid for." She keeps rocking over me, seeking friction, like she can't help herself. I've got a horny beautiful thing on my hands and I reward her by slapping her ass. The sound springs in the car with a loud impact. I do it twice more, giving her a trailer of the spanking she'll get soon. Mabel moans. "Did you have any idea how hot that got me? I fucking love being your provider. Your protector. Your *everything*."

"Now I do." She takes those same nails and rakes them down my sweater-clad torso, biting her kiss-swollen lips. I shudder in pain-pleasure. "And I may not be a damsel in distress, but if there's one man I want by my side, protecting me, sheltering me, being there for me, it's you, Liam. You'll always be it for me too."

We seal the deal with more kisses. It's not long before we're both panting and groaning as Bel grinds over my hard-on like a woman on a mission.

"Take off your dress," I beg, fingers tunnelling through her hair. Our tongues swipe against one another with unison groans. "I want to see you naked when I make you feel good."

Mabel doesn't need to be told twice.

She slips the thin straps off her shoulders and then tugs the blue satin dress off her voluptuous body. The material snags over her chest, making those brown-tipped breasts bounce with the movement.

She drops her dress on the seat next to us.

My vision goes hazy at the arousing sight.

A mass of dark hair falls down her shoulders. Tan skin shines in the golden hour with all of her perfections on display. Blue thong and strappy white heels adorn her otherwise naked form.

I'm rendered speechless by her.

Mabel leans back with a confident smile, letting me drink in her appearance.

I love that she isn't shy.

Enraptured, my fingers have a mind of their own as they map over her curves and stretch marks. Fuck, I just want to devour every inch of this succulent woman. Her love handles—the sexiest thing on a woman. Her generous tits. Her juicy pussy.

I want everything this woman has to give and *more*.

I'll never have enough of her.

Mabel takes my hands in hers and gently places them on her waist. The skin-to-skin contact sears me like a hot poker. "Make me feel good, Liam."

I can't deny this girl anything. I don't want to either.

My fingers slip over her pussy and I learn her contours, roaming over the wetness pouring out of her tight hole before circling her engorged clit. Mabel's moans echo in my mind like a choir. I bring my fingers to my mouth to taste the flavour of her lust.

Sweet.

Tart.

Addicting.

I groan, obsessed with another part of her. "Goddamn, you taste amazing, Bel."

"*Liam.*" She drags my name out like a prayer.

We make out slowly and my fingers return to her cunt. I focus on her greedy clit, loving the way her body reacts to my attention. Trembling with anticipation. Seeking gratification. Rocking as I thrust a finger into her wet heat. Dear God, Bel's eager pussy sucks me down to my last knuckle. She's being such a good girl, running her fingers through my hair and chanting my name in a breathless voice, that I give her a second finger.

Bel's hips buck while I finger her. "Oh, God. Oh, God."

I brush my smile against her lips. It's got a devilish edge to it and she accepts it with a fierce kiss of her own. "Do you like having your pussy played with, *mo ghrá?*"

"Y-Yes." Her arms loop around my neck and she presses her naked body to my fully-clothed one. Something about that arouses me immensely. I like how vulnerable it makes her and how much she trusts me.

The forbidden aspect of being out in the open where the world can see us makes this entire tryst even sexier.

"Dirty, dirty girl," I taunt just as my fingers find a spot deep in Mabel's lush pussy. Her G-spot, no doubt. I give it more love and my girl whimpers, eyes rolling back into her skull. I fucking love seeing her unruly with pleasure. "I knew underneath that sunshine exterior was a filthy, needy brat."

"Oh my God, L-Liam. I'm almost there."

Bel's bouncing tits sway in my face. I snag a pouty brown nipple and suck like a starving man having his first meal after days. My girl moans louder, holding my head to her tits. I'm practically smothered in her cleavage and her sweet fragrance. I love it here. I never want to leave. I want to fucking die here.

I spank her ass for good measure as I keep working her tits with my mouth.

Her pussy clenches around my fingers, growing wetter and making a mess in my lap.

Bel's entire body quakes from the pleasure I wring out.

"We'll get you there, baby," I promise, sucking a hickey on her neck. "You'll never be unsatisfied so long as you're with me."

"You're freakishly good at this," she pants, her eyes narrowing. "Have you had practice?"

The bite of jealousy in her tone has me grinning. This is the first pussy I've touched and it'll be the last one. Mabel doesn't know it, but I'm a virgin.

I've been saving myself for her.

"Are you jealous?" I slap her pussy.

"No. I'm territorial. I don't like knowing there were other women before me. I don't want any of them near you," she says heatedly.

Her words nearly cause me to explode. I continue fingering her—harder—and rubbing her clit—faster. "Don't worry. I'll get 'Property of Mabel' tatted on my skin. That'll scare them away."

"Yes," she hisses, holding my wrist as she rides my fingers. "S-Somewhere very visible, Liam."

"I'll do my forehead."

She laughs mid-moan. "Perfect. So all the girls can know you're *mine*."

You're mine. You're mine. You're mine.

There's no more talking after that declaration.

The moment is now fueled by short, hungry kisses, desperate hands, and dirty words whispered into each other's mouths. The windows are fogged and the smell of lust swirls in the air. I'm playing Mabel like an instrument and she's getting off on every second of it. I pinch her clit and hit her spot with my fingers at the same time.

Over and over again.

Mabel's tightening face as she lets go will forever be embedded in my mind. Head thrown back, lips parted, eyes glazed, my girl gushes all over my hand with her release.

"Liam!" she chokes out my name as she trembles.

When my fingers withdraw from her clamping heat, she shivers at the loss of me. I lick every bit of her wetness from my fingers. "Mm. You're so pretty when you come, baby."

Mabel watches me with a sated expression, caressing my face.

Then she lays her head on my shoulder and hugs me with all her might. I realize physical touch is her love language, and I wrap my arms around her tight, making her feel warm and secure.

"How do you feel?" I ask, kissing her temple.

"Like I've finally come home after years of wandering." Mabel raises her head, gazing into my eyes. "Like everything in my universe feels right once more."

An uncomfortable tightness lodges into my throat. "Bel…"

She kisses my lips feather-soft. "Yes?"

"I'm tired of hiding behind my walls and denying myself the things I want. I couldn't say it before, but I'm saying it now: I want you by my side. Always. As my best friend. As my girl. And one day, as more," I confess softly. "You're mine too, sweetheart. You have been since the first letter. So please, Bel. Say yes and tell me you'll be with me."

Mabel's face morphs with utter happiness and my dream girl finally says, "Yes, Liam. I'll be with you."

I'll be with you.

It's official.

She's mine.

Now everything in my universe is right too.

CHAPTER 10

Mabel

Liam and I are official.

Today marks the fourth week since he asked me to be with him and I said yes.

Four weeks of romantic dates around the city, sweet kisses, comforting hugs, and free-flowing laughter. In the span of such a short time, I've already created so many core memories with my person that I know will last me a lifetime.

I love hanging out in the back seat of his car while I'm wrapped up in his strong arms as he tells me about his career ambitions and life goals. Liam is an open book now. He doesn't hold back anymore and I'm proud of the trusting relationship we've been able to build slowly, brick by brick, over two years.

The letters we wrote the first year sparked our love. The texts we sent the second year fueled our longing. Despite talking all the time, we couldn't communicate the depth of what we felt for one another. Now I know we just needed to see each other in person and deal with our feelings like mature individuals.

I've learned that falling in love doesn't have to be difficult.

It can be as sitting down in front of your significant other and unburdening your heart of all the yearning you feel. It can be as simple as whispering all your secrets and then waiting for them with arms open as they turn their heart over to you forever.

Loving Liam is so simple, it feels like second nature. Loving Liam is so easy, it feels as breathable as the air that keeps me alive.

Loving Liam is everything good that's happened to me and I swear I'll cherish this man until the end of time.

Speaking of my boyfriend, his text comes through just as I'm taking a picture of myself in a dress sent to me by a boutique here in Montardor. Every Tuesday, I like to post an OOTD social media post to support a small business from the city.

> What are you doing this Saturday? —Liam

I snap a quick shot in my mirror, then walk over to my new desk (Liam made it for me from scratch and delivered it last week. It's absolutely perfect.), where I sit and reply to him.

> I think my schedule is booked. —Mabel

It's really not. I'm just playing.

> Oh, yeah? —Liam

> Yeah, I've got a business dinner. It's this musician that's been in my DMs for a while now. He wants me to be the next video vixen in his music video. Asked if I'm down to lie on a piano while he serenades me in a room full of candles. —Mabel

I snicker, just imagining Liam's jealousy. I'm not lying about the musician, but I have zero interest in starring in his music video. However, I do enjoy riling up my boyfriend.

As predicted, a series of explosive text messages arrive.

> Over my dead body. —Liam

> Tell this so-called musician you have a boyfriend that isn't afraid of roughing him up. —Liam

> I swear, Bel. This isn't a threat. It's a fucking promise. —Liam

My mouth salivates at Liam's caveman reaction. He's always so calm, collected, and composed. Not to mention sweet. Since the day we fooled around in his car, I knew he had a dirty side underneath that gentleman exterior.

He just hasn't let me see it again.

And God, I want to see it—be subjected to it—so bad.

I've been horny for a month now. Liam insists we take this 'slow.' Any slower and I think my vagina will decay. I'm ready for Liam to make good on all his naughty promises. I'm ready for us to—pardon my French—fuck and take this relationship to a whole new level.

> I was just teasing you. There's no music video or business dinner happening. —Bel

> You're a brat. —Liam

I bite my bottom lip.

> I know 😊 What are you going to do about it? —Bel

> Guess we'll see on Saturday, babe. —Liam

Okay. Stay calm, Mabel. It's happening.

> What's on Saturday? —Bel

> You and I have a special date. —Liam

I'm about to start hyperventilating. All my prayers are being answered. Hallelujah!

> Can't wait, Lee. <3 —Bel

After a long week, Saturday has arrived and it's our special date in two hours.

My parents already met him three weeks ago when I let it slip that things between my high school pen pal have morphed into *more*. They were always aware that Liam was my best friend, but introducing him as my boyfriend was a whole other ordeal.

I've never dated anyone before, so bringing him home was monumental.

Liam won their hearts with his charming smile and politeness within an hour of having dinner together. My dad and him bonded over their mutual love for the Ravens—Montardor's hockey team—and my mom automatically became his fan when he poured over her cooking like it was the best thing he'd ever eaten.

My parents mean a lot to me. I love that Liam gets along with them.

After I've showered, moisturized, blow-dried my hair in waves, and applied my go-to date night glam, I pack an overnight bag since I'll be sleeping over at Liam's place tonight. His parents are out of town and we have the entire house to ourselves.

Liam hasn't outright said what this 'special date' is, but I have a feeling it's going to end with us naked, between the sheets.

I change into my lingerie set—a lacy red bra with matching high-cut panties—and wear black opaque stockings with a grey knit minidress. It's late November now, so the weather has gotten significantly colder. My outfit is complete with a beige coat and thigh-high boots that make my legs appear longer than ever. Since I got a fresh set of burgundy nails—courtesy of my hard-working boyfriend who loves to spend money on me—I slip on a few gold knuckle rings and hoop earrings.

My phone buzzes with a text message. Liam says he's downstairs. I could have driven myself to his place, but my boyfriend is a bit old-fashioned in that regard—he likes to pick me up and drive me around. I sense it has something to do with him feeling like my protector and provider.

When I step out into the fall evening, I see him coming out from the driver's side, a huge bouquet of red roses in his hands.

There's a pink tinge to his cheeks. From seeing me or the cold weather, we'll never know.

I cross halfway to him and his eyes trek from my boots to the top of my black hair with an appreciative glance. I do the same to him. He's in dark slacks, a black button-down, and a grey king-sized coat that fits him like a dream.

Liam O'Connell is perfection and I want to spend tonight proving it to him.

"Hi." I smile cheekily when he stops in front of me.

"Hey." He leans down to peck my lips softly. His beard tickles me. "This is for you. The florist didn't have any sunflowers, so I hope these will do."

It melts my heart that he stops at the florist every time before a date to spoil me with flowers.

Best. Boyfriend. Ever.

"I love them, Liam. Thank you." I take the bouquet from his hands and kiss him again, lingering longer. I love kissing him. I can kiss him all day and night and never get bored. "I also got you a gift, but I'd like to give it to you later, if that's all right?"

His eyes narrow playfully, falling to the big purse slung over my shoulder. He knows where I keep the goods hidden. "You didn't have to get me anything, Bel."

"Consider it a one-month anniversary gift then." I kiss his cold cheek. "Are we ready to go?"

He weaves our gloved hands together and leads me to the passenger side of the car, opening the door for me. I climb in and he presses a kiss to my knuckles before closing the door.

The car smells like him—clean, masculine, and pinewood—and his scent stirs the butterflies in my stomach. I've been anticipating this date all week long and now that we're here, I'm equal parts nervous and excited.

"You look beautiful," Liam rasps once he settles behind the wheel.

We might both be newbies when it comes to this whole relationship thing, but I think we're doing pretty good for ourselves, if I do say so myself. There's something humbling in navigating through this 'first time' together and I love that we meet each other halfway.

"And you look handsome as ever, Liam." I close the distance until our lips speak what our hearts cannot say yet.

Liam takes me to *La Flamme* for dinner, a restaurant on the East Side that's notorious for being one of the best date night spots. I keep a list in my phone of all the new places I want to try out and clearly he's done his research.

We're on our way back to his home and those butterflies from earlier? They've tripled and are having a party inside my belly. I'm playing with the roses in my lap while Liam's thumb is rubbing the back of my hand in soothing circles. It's like he can sense the slight tension and he's doing his best to set me at ease.

It strikes me that Liam too might be nervous.

"I had a great time, Liam," I say over the sound of a Zayn Malik song. "Much more fun than I would have had with that musician."

His nostrils flare and his jaw tightens.

I barely hide my evil smile.

"You keep mentioning him, Bel, and I'm going to have to do something about it."

"What are you going to do?" My voice is inexplicably hoarse.

Please, do something about it, Liam.

"You'll see soon enough," he says gruffly, his voice a sensual threat. He releases my hand and goes for my thigh, squeezing it. "I have plans for you."

My eyes widen when Liam's thick fingers slip to my inner thigh.

"What kind of plans?" I ask breathlessly.

"I'd rather show you." Liam's fingers swim over the juncture of my thighs, pressing over my stocking-covered pussy like a warning. "Now be a good girl and behave until we get home."

Oh my God. "And if I don't?"

"Then I'll have to pull over to the side of the road and give your ass the spanking it deserves."

Liam shocks the hell out of me with those filthy words. Not that I'm complaining. I just fall completely mum, like the good girl he asked me to be, until we make it to his place.

There's no sign of the jealous caveman when he parks his SUV in the driveway of a quaint two-storey, red-brick house.

Any other day, I would have admired it a little bit longer. Now I'm faced with the giddiness somersaulting in my system as Liam goes around his car and comes to my door.

He helps me out, his easy-going smile fixed in place.

His intense eyes give him away, though. He feels the strong energy crackling between us like a live-wire.

Liam picks up my overnight bag and ushers us to the porch.

Be calm, Bel. Don't jump his bones. Yet.

Liam unlocks the front door. "After you, Mabel."

I enter before him, my spine straightening to attention as his warmth closes in behind my back. I know he's just locking the door, but I swear it feels like we're seconds aways from slicing the sexual tension. It started brewing when Liam decided to eye-fuck me in that restaurant.

Talk about foreplay.

"This is nice," I say to no one in particular. The air is laced with a potpourri-like aroma that's quintessentially fall. Apple. Cinnamon. Cozy. It only heightens the sensuality of the moment. "You have a lovely place."

Liam's lips find residence at my ear. His warm breath splays against the side of my neck as he murmurs, "Take off your coat."

I don't even want to think of the state of my panties. If he keeps talking low in that deep, borderline indecent voice of his, they'll be incinerated in no time. "O-Okay."

He helps me out of my coat, his knuckles brushing my arms as he plants a kiss against my pulse point before inhaling my scent. My knees almost buckle. "Jesus, you smell so good."

"Last I checked, the name on my birth certificate is Mabel Lani Garcia, but I guess I can change it to Jesus if you prefer."

He chuckles and swats my ass. "You got jokes tonight, eh? Get moving. Second door down the hallway is my room."

My heart thunders in response, but I pretend to mock-pout. "You don't want to give me a house tour? You know, MTV crib style."

Liam shrugs off his own coat and deposits it on a hanger inside the closet by the entryway. Then he advances my way like a man on a mission. "I would, but you and I both know you aren't interested in a tour."

I fist the collar of his button-down as he nears. "No, I'm not." Instead of kissing him, I let our lips brush against one another. "But you know what I'm interested in? Dessert, Liam."

The smirk on his face is confident. Arrogant. Devastating. I love it. "I already told you once. Be a good girl and I'll give you anything you want, baby."

"What if I don't want to be a good girl?"

"You want to hear a secret?"

I nod slowly.

Liam's lips skirt over my jaw and he whispers, "I don't actually want you to be one either. I like it when you're bad, Bel. Really, really, fucking bad."

Speechless. Words have escaped me. My entire vocabulary has been reduced to a 'puh' sound that leaves my parted lips.

Sweet and shy Liam is the best.

But shameless and dirty-talking Liam? Oh, we're about to have so much fun tonight.

Taking advantage of my silenced state, Liam's hands grab handfuls of my ass and rope me into his big body. "The night's not over yet and I have plans for you." His commanding tone causes my pussy to throb. "Now go to my room and get comfortable. I'll be with you in a moment."

Liam releases me like he hasn't set me on fire with those words. I blink, disoriented, hot, and well, ready to get it on. "U-Uh, right. I'll just go…do that."

He simply winks and walks in the opposite direction, turning on the hallway lights as he goes towards…the kitchen?

I, on the other hand, grab my bag and follow his instructions dutifully.

Second door on the right of the hallway greets me. I twist open the doorknob and flick on the light switch before entering.

Hunter green walls, pecan brown flooring, sandy beige accents. The colour palette in Liam's room reminds me of a dark enchanting fairy-tale forest, which I suppose is quite on brand for my fantasy-reading boyfriend. The star of the show isn't the queen-sized bed with fresh sheets and large pillows fit for cuddling. It's the wooden bookshelf tucked against a wall containing rows of colourful book spines.

Without a shadow's doubt, Liam built this bookshelf himself.

And as my fingers graze a shelf, a smile blooms over my face. I'm so ridiculously proud of this guy. How many girlfriends can say their boyfriends genuinely know how to create beautiful furniture pieces from scratch? Not many, I presume.

The floor beneath my feet is spotless and there appears to be not a speck of dust in the air. Have I mentioned Liam is a true clean freak? This guy stocks up on cleaning supplies the same way girls do on makeup products. He once told me that every week, like clockwork, he wipes down his entire room so it looks straight out of an AD magazine.

My smile grows even more as I belatedly notice the helium balloons floating near his bedside end table, labelled '*Happy 1 month anniversary,*' and the twinkling lights he's garlanded around the room to create an ambiance for us.

Liam's turned his entire room into a romantic little getaway.

I'm totally swooning.

I place my bag on the floor and pad over to his ensuite. I take a moment to pop a breath mint, reapply my dark red lipstick, and wash my hands thoroughly because no one should get intimate without doing so prior.

I also assess my reflection one more time in the mirror and conclude I look banging.

Liam's going to faint once he sees my lingerie.

Going back into his room, I make myself at home by plopping onto his bed. I'll have to ask what kind of fabric softener Liam uses because it

THE GUY FOR ME

smells divine. His own cologne lingers in the sheets, and I inhale a greedy gulp like an addict getting her fix.

Slow footsteps echo along the hallway. I perk up and lie sideways on his bed, propping myself up on one elbow.

Liam strolls into the bedroom like a larger-than-life king entering his court. Except instead of the proverbial sword, he's carrying a…wooden board?

He nears and I finally register the contents. Oh, my. The charcuterie board is layered with a multitude of chocolates, brownies, and fruits. He wasn't kidding about dessert.

Liam chuckles when he notices the stars in my eyes and the drool at the corner of my lips. "Hi."

"Hi, right back at you." I scoot on the bed to make space for him to gingerly deposit the board. "That looks delicious. Did you make it?"

Liam comes to lie behind me. He slings an arm around my waist and pulls me back so we're fitted together like a puzzle.

I love being held by him like this.

Liam drops a tender kiss on my cheek, lingering to nuzzle my cheek some more. "Yes, I did. I watched a YouTube video and prepped it this afternoon."

Get you a boyfriend who knows how to satisfy your sweet tooth cravings.

I snag a brownie from the bunch, trying to mask my teasing grin. "Time to add professional chef to your résumé, Bob the Builder."

I burst out laughing when he takes it upon himself to tickle me, his face shoved into my neck. I try to twist away from him, but I'm trapped in his embrace. It's okay, though. I don't ever want to leave it.

"Call me Bob the Builder one more time. I dare you," he growls playfully, nibbling my earlobe when my tickle-induced laughing fit finally subsides.

I feed him a peace offering. The rest of my brownie. Liam makes sure to lick my fingers clean of chocolate traces. Why is that so sexy to me? I swear my ovaries are shaking.

"I really like what you've done with your room." I wiggle my eyebrows.

His eyes soften. "Happy one month, babe."

"Is it crazy to say that it feels like a lot longer?"

He pushes a lock of my hair behind my ear. "In my mind, you've been mine for two years, Bel."

"Ditto," I whisper and the megawatt smile on his face gleams bright like a diamond.

Liam kisses the tip of my nose—physical touch is my love language and the fact that he showers me with it at every opportunity makes my heart so happy—and reaches for a remote, switching on the TV mounted on his wall.

In ten seconds flat, *The Vampire Diaries* plays on the screen. I gasp. "Are we really watching this?"

"You once mentioned wanting to have a marathon. I figured we could start at the beginning and talk about how perfect human Elena and vampire Stefan were for each other."

A man after my own heart. "For the record, this is the best date ever."

"For the record"—Liam snags a banana piece with a toothpick and dips it into a bowl of melted chocolate, then takes a bite—"I know this is the best date ever."

Liam has gained a lot of confidence in the last month and I love to hear it in his words, love to see it in his actions, just love it. Period. He's still his usual shy, quiet self (I don't see that ever changing nor would I want that because it's part of his essence), but he's more open now with his jokes and flirting.

I snuggle deeper into his body, backing my tush against his lap. His sharp intake of breath makes me grin. "All right, *Bob*, let's get this party started."

The next two hours are spent watching *The Vampire Diaries* and sharing commentary like we're paid critics, while polishing the dessert board. I *ooh* and *aah* over the Salvatore brothers, Elena's gorgeous hair, and how I'd love to spend a day in the fictional town of Mystic Falls. Rewatching the show from the beginning, Liam and I both agree that Caroline had the best character development and that selfless Bonnie deserved so much better.

With every passing episode, Liam seems to tug me impossibly closer until I can't say where we begin and where we end. The low flame sizzling in my core rises into an inferno. After concluding the third episode, I graze my lips against the light scar on Liam's cheek. "I have a gift for you."

The undertone of lust flashes in his blue eyes, but I see him trying to maintain the gentlemanly façade. While I do have *that* kind of gift for him, I want to show him what I spent days scouring the internet to secure.

"Show me." His voice is a gruff purr. He may as well have said 'Fuck me' with the way my body reacts to those two words.

My bag is resting on the floor beside his bed. I scoot forward, well aware that it puts my ass in a perilous position for Liam's roaming hands. The hem of my short knit dress rides higher.

Liam groans under his breath.

My smirk is victorious.

I pluck the wrapped gift from my bag and turn back to Liam, so I'm kneeling on the bed next to his reclined frame. "Here."

Liam takes it from my hands, unable to keep the excitement from curling his lips. He's silent for a moment as he weighs the gift, evaluating the shape. "Is this a book?"

"My lips are sealed. It wouldn't be a surprise if I told you." I pretend to zip my mouth and shoot the imaginary key away.

He takes out the little card I wrote him with the '*Happy One Month Anniversary*' message, curving his thumb over the writing in reverence. I know how much he cherishes my written words but seeing him now, I'm beginning to imagine his expressions when he'd read my letters.

I would have melted into a puddle if I'd seen the tender smile Liam is currently sporting.

I've always considered myself a headstrong, independent girl who doesn't need someone to complete me. I strongly believe that no one out there needs another person to feel whole—you already are—yet Liam with his gentleness, soft heart, and kind mannerism calls out to something deep within me. I realize now that even those who are fully whole can have soul mates beyond themselves. Ones who understand and accept them as they are, flaws and perfections, and make life an adventure worth living.

Liam is that for me.

My kindred spirit.

My soul companion.

I'm floored by the realization, while he's unaware of the magnitude of my thoughts as he tears open the package.

Can he see on my face how altered I feel?

Before I can speak, he murmurs, "Bel...you didn't."

My cheeks warm under the potency of his amazed expression. Like Liam, I like to provide for my loved ones too. Now I'm getting the impression that he's not used to being given much, that even when he gets a *little*, he lights up like a little kid on Christmas morning.

I'm not sure if I should burst into tears or be joyful.

In his hands, my boyfriend is holding the first edition of *The Fellowship of the Ring*, hardback and printed in the 1950s. He's read his paperback copy over ten times. The spine is entirely cracked. Since he enjoyed the story so much, I figured he should have this version. One he could proudly showcase on his bookshelf.

"I did." I bite my lip. "Do you like it?"

His fingers touch the book like it's the most precious memorabilia ever. "This is the best gift I've ever gotten. I can't believe you did this for me."

"I'd do anything for you."

Without glancing away from me, Liam puts the book on the nightstand and cradles my face. I gravitate towards him like it's the most natural thing. "I'd do anything for you too, Bel."

My heart soars like a thousand doves taking flight.

Closing the distance, our mouths finally meet.

No feeling in the world can compare to kissing Liam. It always starts slow and sensual and transforms into fast and demanding like a wave that overtakes your being. You're helpless to go with the current. A sea of bliss and our lips cling to one another like ship-wrecked lovers.

"Liam," I moan when his tongue teases the seam of my mouth. His hands are going from my waist, to my rib cage, to my heavy breasts. Fondling my nipples over my sweater dress and starting the trip all over again. My libido is on fire. "I need you."

Liam releases my lips, breathing hard. His chest bows underneath my hands. "You want me?"

His tone is laced with a hint of apprehension. If I wasn't aware of Liam's fear of rejection and insecurity, I might have assumed he was playing hard to get because it's been a month that we've been kissing and grinding and never crossing past second base.

But I know how much words—reassurance—matter to him.

I nod desperately, digging my fingers into the collar of his dress shirt. "Yes, Liam. Please. I can't even think straight anymore. I need you inside of me. *Now*."

His hard-on is poking my thigh like a greenlight. "Fuck, Bel. I want you too. Down to my bones, I ache with need for you."

A zing of gratification lights my nerve endings.

This is going to happen.

We're finally going to make love.

I attack his clothes with enthusiasm, but Liam hastily grabs my hands. "W-Wait. L-Let me close the lights."

I pause, frowning. "Why would we shut the lights?"

His blue eyes are veneered with desire, but there's a vulnerable edge too.

I can practically see the wheels in his mind churning as he attempts to say it.

Suddenly, it hits me.

It took me years to build my confidence and to feel comfortable in my skin. Now? I love myself and the way I look. But I'm not so daft to assume that Liam's perception of himself has changed from the second we started dating. He's still insecure about the way he looks, given the way he's been treated in his past. It pains me that his bullies have led him to believe he isn't attractive or worthy.

I promise, even if it's the last thing I do, I'm going to make sure this man knows how beautiful he is inside and out.

I curve my palm over his bearded jaw and smile, even as my heart batters a rough rhythm against my chest. I wish I could go back in time and hurt every motherfucker who had something mean to say about my best friend. "Liam, I want to see our bodies and everything we do to each other. Please don't turn off the lights."

"Okay," he whispers with defeat.

That won't do. He's only going to leave them on to please me. Not because he's comfortable.

Never letting my smile waver, I get up and extend a hand.

Confused, he takes it and rises to his full six-foot-five height. Shifting on his feet with uncertainty. Smoothing a palm over his clothes so they're less askew—thanks to my grabby hands.

"C'mere." My destination is a full-length mirror next to his bookshelf. I drag him along and he follows dutifully. I position Liam in front and watch the way his Adam's apple bobs. I glue myself to his side and meet his gaze in the mirror. "Do you trust me?"

"With my entire being."

I press a kiss to his sturdy bicep. "What do you see when you look in the mirror, Liam?"

He takes a deep breath and lets it out in a slow whistling exhale, shaking his head like he's trying to get rid of his bad thoughts. "Babe, you don't want to know."

The smile falls off my face. "Liam..."

His stare is downcast. "Why don't you tell me what *you* see?"

I wanted to do a little exercise in self-love, but now I'm on the verge of tears. How did the world convince this amazing human being that he's anything less than stellar?

"You want to know what I see?" I hold his chin and bring his face back up so our gazes meet again. "The prettiest shade of blue. I've never seen more lovely eyes, Liam."

"I love yours too," he chokes out.

"You have great hair. Soft and thick. I love running my hands through it." I do it to prove my point. The stylish backcomb is now messy, his strands flopping over his forehead endearingly. "Don't even get me started on your beard."

I'm ashamed to admit how many times I've imagined the feel of it as he eats my pussy out. A girl can dream, right?

"What else?" he demands and my suspicions are confirmed.

My boyfriend has a praise kink.

I'm going to feed it so well.

"You have wonderful skin, courtesy of Mabel and all her skincare recommendations." We chuckle in unison and then he sobers up when I stare at him with a serious glint. I lean my head against his shoulder. "Liam, you're so handsome and you don't even know it."

"Thank you," he returns, twisting his face to kiss the top of my head. "I...believe you, Bel."

That statement gives me the courage I need to continue my appraisal.

Grabbing hold of his arms, I twist his body so we're face-to-face. My hand skims the collar of his black dress shirt and I finger the first button, peering up at him. "Do you still trust me?"

Tension balloons in the space between us before Liam closes his eyes briefly and nods earnestly. "Yes. Always."

The weight of those two words settles on my soul. I don't take his trust lightly or for granted. It means more to me than I can put into words.

Ever so slowly, I begin to undo his buttons until his chest is revealed.

Liam is doing everything in his power not to meet my gaze.

I push the dress shirt off his shoulders. It lands in a pool by our feet. Liam's fists are balled by his sides and his eyes cut into the air above my head, like he's scared of my reaction.

I suck in a sharp breath.

Holy fucking shit.

I need a moment.

"My God, Liam," I murmur, awestruck. "You're...There are no words."

Liam O'Connell is nothing short of astonishing. Tall, powerful, and so *thick*, I'm stunned at the sight he paints. His skin is paler than mine and he has a light dusting of dark brown hair that heightens his masculinity. My fingers go to his rounded belly and move towards his love handles, caressing every beautiful inch of him. Those emotive eyes of his follow my movements like he's bewitched as I drag my hands up his chest, feeling his heart thundering beneath my palm. I move to his brawny arms, which evoke the feeling of home when he wraps them around me securely.

I'm a big girl, but standing in front of him, I feel small and protected.

I complete my journey by looping my forearms around his neck.

Our eyes meet and I see a thousand questions swimming in Liam's blue depths.

My sexy, battle-hardened warrior.

"You're perfect," I finally declare with utmost sincerity. "Absolutely perfect—"

Before I can complete my sentence, Liam kisses me hard and presses his forehead to mine, shivering gently. He's absorbing my truth and doing his damnedest not to let his demons win.

"We all have good and bad days, Liam. No one wakes up every morning *always* loving the way they look. I too have days where I don't feel my best and that's okay. We are human after all. Self-love is about accepting and respecting yourself. It's about appreciating all our flaws and strength— mental, physical, emotional—and not comparing yourself to a standard the world has set out. It's about treating yourself with kindness and realizing your worth. There is no one like you on this Earth and I wish you'd see what I see when I look at you. Unrefined beauty that takes my breath away. You're priceless, Liam O'Connell. Please don't ever forget it."

A storm of emotions plays across his face. Shell-shock. Gratitude. Pure, unadulterated glee.

Liam tightens his arms around me, a silent message that states he's keeping me forever. He has nothing to worry about. I'm never leaving him.

"How did I get so lucky and find a girl like you?" he rasps with wonder. "How is it that the universe knew exactly what I needed and brought you into my life at a time when I felt so hopeless? I don't know what I did to deserve you, but I plan on spending the rest of my life making you the happiest woman."

Hell, maybe I have a praise kink too because now I'm staring at him with unabashed joy. "Liam…"

"I promise I'm going to do my best every day to see myself in a better light. Not just for you, but for myself because…I deserve it," he says hesitantly and I nod in encouragement. "And I want to live a life where I'm confident and self-accepting of all the things that make me…*me*."

Yes, yes, yes. This is what I want for him too. "I'll be here every step of the way for you. I swear it, Liam."

"Kiss me," he whispers. "And let's forget about the world. I'm ready to lose myself in you."

CHAPTER 11

Mabel

"I'm a virgin," Liam murmurs against my lips when we pull apart for air. "Does that bother you?"

The thought that I'll be Liam's first makes me so hot. I'm picturing his face in the throes of passion as he learns what it's like to fuck—hard, fast, slow—and feel my silk wrapped around his hardness. Will he be a quiet or a loud lover? Will he be gentle or downright rough? I can't wait to learn it all.

"That you're a virgin? No. I'm practically coming at the prospect of popping your cherry."

"I want to meet your expectations, Bel. I don't want to disappoint you."

I tear open his belt, pull it out of the loops, and drop it to the floor. Next, I attack the button of his black slacks. My skin is vibrating with the need to see all of him, including that impressive cock that I've only ever felt as we grinded in the back seat of his car. "I can assure you, Liam, anything you do to me, I'm going to like. My expectations have rarely been met. If there's one guy who can rock my world right, it's you."

"How many guys have there been before me?"

I don't register the hard edge in his tone. I'm so focused on getting his pants off so I can see his briefs and—holy hell. Liam. Is. Packing. My eyes widen and I sputter. That has to be an easy eight-incher. Or nine. Shit, maybe even ten. My pussy clenches. Out of fear or excitement? Who knows.

Liam suddenly grabs my jaw and redirects my face to his. I gasp, caught off guard by the roughness but also…loving it. "How many guys have there been before me, baby?" Fire burns in his gaze as he repeats his question.

I goad him like a brat, "Why, are you jealous?"

He's *so* jealous and I love it.

Liam leans down and the ends of his hair trickle over my forehead. His breath fans my kiss-swollen lips as he taunts, "I'm going to fuck you so good tonight, you'll forget you ever spread these thick thighs for any motherfucker before me."

It's official. I've gone speechless.

Dirty-talking Liam has entered the chat.

A guy who's sweet outside of the bedroom, but a complete beast inside of it? Sign me up.

"Walk the talk, Liam," I taunt back. "Make me forget there was anyone else before you."

"Fuck." Liam drags my mouth to his for a searing kiss, holding me by the neck. "You're feisty."

"What are you going to do about it?"

"Give you a mouthful of cock if you don't behave."

Can you orgasm with just words? I think I came a little in my thong from the deep, suave way he imposed authority. "Bring it on."

There's a smug glint in his gaze as he accepts my challenge, shoulders rolling back like a proud king about to bask in his victory.

Liam's lips latch onto my neck as he delivers a series of open-mouth kisses. Some ending in nips. Others in sucking love bites. I'm panting from the pleasure of it all.

He shoves my opaque stockings and panties down to my knees and I use my feet to kick them off all the way, while he pushes my grey knit dress up to my waist, dislodging from my neck long enough to tear it off my body in one swipe.

It lands on the floor next to the rest of our discarded items.

I'm left in nothing but my super sexy red bra.

In the background, I hear Stefan and Damon arguing. Guess we forgot to turn off the show.

Except I can't communicate that to Liam because my throat has dried up like the Sahara Desert when I catch the ravenous look on his face. Like he'll die if he doesn't get a taste of me.

He's helplessly fixed in place by my near naked body.

I do him a favour and unhook my bra, throwing it on the floor as well. Now I'm truly in my birthday suit.

Liam's eyes do a slow sweep of my heaving breasts, my rounded stomach, my generous hips, and my long legs. Not a single stitch of my curvaceous body is left untouched when he's done. The way he grazes my stretch marks with his fingertips in adoration nearly brings tears to my eyes.

He hasn't said it yet, but I feel it in my bones.

This man loves me with his entire being.

Liam inhales a quick prayer and shakes his head in disbelief. "You're exquisite, Mabel. A dream come to life."

I close the distance.

Both of us groan at the slide of naked skin against each other. Liam lifts me into his arms with ease and I wrap my legs and arms around him. He carries me to his bed and tosses me on the soft bedding, like he's a soldier returning from war and I'm the maiden he's chosen to slake his sexual appetite.

Grabbing the remote, Liam turns off the TV—we were just at the scene where Stefan was consoling Elena—and grabs the back of my knees, pulling me down to the edge of the bed and splitting my legs wide-open. "Spread for me, sweetheart. I want to give your pussy a kiss."

Oh my goodness.

He's already lowering his face to my most intimate flesh. A wave of insecurity hits me. I'm waxed, moisturized, and groomed down there, yet I don't have a pretty pink porn star pussy. I know, I know. Vaginas come in all shapes and forms, but now I'm the one worried about meeting Liam's 'expectations.'

I rise up on my elbows, my stomach dipping, to get a better view of the situation. "Listen, Liam—"

But said insecurity flies out the window as Liam's impatient tongue licks my wet slit. Once, experimentally. Twice, for my flavour. Thrice, because he's hooked. His eyes roll into his skull and he groans like he just tasted the sweetest candy.

"Goddammit, Bel," he growls. "Your scent. Your taste. Your pussy. So fucking nice, baby."

We've barely begun and my heart is racing the way it does when I'm near orgasming.

Liam swings my legs over his strapping shoulders and uses his fingers to pry my pussy open for his feasting. "Tell me what you like, okay? I only want to please you."

"I-I will."

I don't have the chance to tell him I've never had my pussy eaten before he fastens onto me. That the two guys I previously had sex with were of the *wham, bam, thank you ma'am* variety. Meaning a little bit of fingering and thrusting their cocks for two minutes was their idea of sex. I rolled with it, considering I did have a bit of fun. But neither wanted to eat me out and quite frankly, I didn't want their mouths near my pussy either. Sex was one thing, but the act of oral always felt much more intimate to me.

Liam is passing with flying colours.

If he hadn't admitted his inexperience to me, I would have assumed this guy held a certificate of excellence in pussy eating because goddamn is he licking me for broke.

I have no choice but to throw my head back and moan loudly. "*Liam.*"

My temperature rises until I'm a furnace. Heat rushes through my veins. My toes curl, my fists ball in my sheet, and my entire body twists as Liam works me to a fast release. He's got his middle finger screwing my pussy while his tongue hugs my clit like they're reunited best friends. His rough exhales warm my flesh. His mouth slurps my wetness like it's his main source of nourishment. And his beard is a constant wonderful friction over my sensitive skin.

The cherry on top of the cake is the way Liam is groaning, like licking my pussy isn't for my pleasure. It's for *his.*

He's gone feral after one taste, his fingers digging into my thighs while he smothers his face in my pussy. My cum is all over the tip of his nose, his lips, his chin, his beard. "Fuck, if I knew you were walking around with this smooth cunt hidden underneath your panties, I'd have knocked on your door months ago, Bel."

"L-Liam, please." My thighs are shaking on either side of him. "Please, please, please."

His lips return where they belong: suctioning my clit. When his tongue joins the mix and starts flicking it in a quick rhythm, my soul leaves my body.

I retract my earlier statement. Some men are good at opening jars *and* eating pussy.

My fingers knot in his hair and I buck my hips against his face. I'm reduced to a boneless heap of desperation, neediness, and loud moans.

Liam groans when my fingers rake through his scalp. From the pain. From the pleasure. From the fact that my burgundy nails are paid and provided by him.

"Fuckkk." He tongues me faster. Fingers me harder. Drives me wilder. "You taste so fucking delicious. God, I just want to put you on your back with your knees to your chest and make your wet pussy take every inch of my cock like a horny bad girl."

I'm about to say *Liam, please do*, but the only thing that comes out of my mouth are moans that grow louder exponentially by the second.

The sensation of Liam's swirling tongue and his fingers moving in and out of me, making love to my G-spot, ignite my body like a flame.

My climax rushes out of me as ecstasy sizzles through my veins.

Still relishing in my ground-breaking orgasm, I glance down to see Liam raising his head. His eyes meet mine. Intoxicated, they stare at me like I'm the sole reason for his air.

And his beard…

Dear, Lord, my cum glistens on it like a prized commodity.

I sure soaked it like the 'naughty little bad girl' he teased me for being.

"Are you okay?" he asks hoarsely, maintaining eye contact as he peppers kisses over my inner thighs, my satisfied pussy, the stretch marks on my lower stomach. "Was that fine?"

"Fine?" I smile with a lazy grin. "Liam, you made me come so hard, I think I forgot what year it is."

He chuckles. The sound vibrates through my sensitive body. He lowers my thighs from his shoulders and kneads my muscles. I don't miss the way he traces the dimples absentmindedly with his finger, connecting them like a constellation. "Glad to hear you enjoyed it."

I narrow my eyes as he kisses his way up my body, my breathing still laboured. "I thought you said you were a virgin. Where did you learn to do that?"

Liam teasingly nips my jaw, then husks in my ear, "I said I'm a virgin. Not a saint."

"Have you given head to other girls before?" If he says yes, I'm going to turn green with envy like the Hulk. I'm just as possessive of him as he is of me.

A half-smirk curves his lips. "Nah. I've just spent hours watching porn and reading those smutty novels you like so I can prepare myself for you."

His eagerness to please me makes me even happier than ever. My arms square around his shoulders and I draw him to my mouth for kisses. "Wow." *Kiss.* "Just know." *Kiss.* "That I'm giving you." *Kiss.* "An imaginary gold star." *Kiss.* "For how well you performed."

Liam plunders his tongue into my mouth, making me taste myself. Oh, he's so kinky. "Thank you, sweetheart."

As we continue to make out, Liam molds his body to mine. Burly. Unyielding. Comforting. Home. He feels wonderful. I caress his beefy arms, his hair-roughened torso, his broad back—namely his tattooed spine—and his bubble butt over his white briefs.

Ready and hard, his cock is stamped between us.

I imagine the size, the texture, the scent of it, and I'm salivating.

"Liam." I sigh when he draws his warm kisses down to my neck.

"Every time you'd post a picture wearing a bikini or lingerie, I'd wonder what these would look like." Liam licks his lips while staring at my tits. "What they would feel like." He grabs handfuls of them. I moan. "What they would taste like." Giving me a mischievous smile, his tongue darts out to lave my brown nipples and he groans, eyes closing. "And they're better than anything I could have imagined."

Liam wastes no time and gets straight to work again, alternating between licking, sucking, and pinching my pebbled nipples. There's something animalistic in the way he never gazes away from me, evaluating my reactions to see what I like and filing it away for later use. He's so fascinated by every bit of me. Completely addicted and we haven't even gotten to the main course.

He's so fucking hot.

I'm chanting his name while he works me to another fevered pitch. Can you come just by having your breasts played with? I guess we won't find out, considering Liam also slips two fingers back into my pussy and finger-fucks me once more.

"You're almost there, Bel, I can feel you tightening," he rasps, thumb polishing my clit. "You like me playing with your pussy, hm?"

I nod, unable to form words.

"Of course you do," he says devilishly and kisses me with tongue. "Is this what you'd picture when you'd touch yourself at night to the thought of me?"

I whimper in reply.

He chuckles darkly. "Naughty, naughty girl. Now come for me. Come all over my fingers so I can lick them clean."

It only takes a few more dirty words, a few more finger strokes, a few more sucks on my nipples.

I let go with a loud, shaking moan.

I've never exploded so fast in my life. Not even with my sparkly pink dildo.

My face is flushed, the hairs around my face sweaty, and my body floats on another dimension.

As promised, Liam pulls his wet fingers out of my pussy and sucks them down to his knuckles. "I'll never have enough of you, babe."

Panting, I frame his face with my two hands. "Liam, I need you in my mouth."

His eyes flash dangerously and he whispers back, "You sure?"

"Yes." To prove my point, I drag my manicured fingernails over the bulge in his briefs. "I'm dying to see it."

Dying to open my mouth and hoover the cum out of his cock. It's the least he deserves for not only giving me one, but two life-altering orgasms. Plus, I want to suck him off. Badly.

There's a slight moment of hesitation as he glances down at his briefs and then at my mouth. Inquisitively. As though wondering if I can actually fit him in my mouth.

Decision made, he gets off the bed and comes to stand by the edge of it. I automatically go into a kneeling position before him, holding my breath for the moment he takes off his last shred of clothing.

Liam bites his bottom lip and toys with the waistband of his white briefs. "Listen, if at any moment you want to stop, just tell me, okay?"

I smile lovingly as he shoves down his briefs. "I won't want to stop— *holy fuck!*"

His cock springs free.

I gasp out loud.

And then fall into utter shock.

His cock is girthy with a bulbous tip that's already leaking pre-cum. Not to mention, I was right. He's somewhere between the eight-nine-inch mark. Forget my vagina, I'm not even sure I'll be able to fit him inside my mouth. Crap, can I even close my fingers around it?

Seeing my moon-eyed expression, Liam's brows furrow in concern.

"Mabel?"

I shake my head and snap out of it.

Oh my God.

"Liam, I'm so sorry, but that's not a cock. That's a fucking rifle!" I cry out. "You just walk around all day with that thing shoved in your pants?"

He throws his head back and howls with booming laughter. "Is that a hypothetical question?"

I'm not new to sucking dick. I've done it about five times.

But never in my life have I sucked such a huge one.

"That's a porn-worthy cock, Liam. Actually, scratch that. I don't think I've ever seen one as humongous as yours even in a porn video. At least, not the ones I've come across. Not that I watch a lot of porn, of course. Because I don't. I was just curious that one time." I'm rambling now while mentally calculating if I can properly jerk him off with two hands. "Shit, all I'm trying to say is that, well, you are *blessed*. And I'm a little bit worried about how we'll fit."

Liam's laughter slowly dies down, but the elated glimmer in his eyes never disperses.

He cups my chin and strokes his thumb over my jaw before brushing his lips to mine. "You've grinded in my lap for the past month. Learned its shape and size. Don't act like you didn't know it would be massive, Bel. I'm a big boy and I've got a big cock. And you're going to take every inch like a good girl tonight, aren't you, baby?"

My pussy throbs at his words.

You're going to take every inch like a good girl tonight, aren't you, baby?

Pushing aside my worries, I nod with renewed determination. "Hell yeah, I'm going to take it."

He beams and it warms me like the heat of the sun.

I take the scrunchie off my wrist and tie my hair back. "Is this your first time getting a blow job?"

He chin-tips, a pink blush on his cheeks. "Yes. I've been saving myself for you."

"That might be one of the sexiest things I've ever heard." My heart does a happy jig. I like that I'm the first (and last) girl who gets to show this gentle giant so much pleasure. "You're going to love this, Lee."

Liam rumbles his approval when my fingers wrap around his fully erect cock. It's hot and steely. The sight of my nails grazing the topside causes him to let loose a full-body shiver.

Blinking at him coyly, I get on all fours and lean forward to flick my tongue against his flared tip. "Mhm."

Liam's hands come to cup my face and his jaw slackens. "*Fuckkk.*"

Emboldened by his response, I open my mouth wider and suck him in. He tastes a hint salty, a touch of musk, and something that triggers a primal instinct in me. Liam releases a hoarse, "Bel," laced with the deepest desire, and that twists the last cog that sets me into motion.

I turn into a mad, sexually-driven woman in the pursuit of making her boyfriend lose his voice from groaning her name. Wanting to see his face transform as he dangles on the edge of frenzy and then tightens once he inevitably crosses it.

My head bobs up and down as I shuttle inches of his cock in and out of my mouth.

Liam's too long, too thick. I can't take all of him yet. It'll take some practice before I can deep-throat him. For now, I lick the underside of his shaft, squeeze his balls, spit on his length, and suck as much of him as I can while my hands work in tandem. I'm having one helluva good time slobbering on his cock and beating it with fast strokes. The thought that it's mine—he's mine—has more arousal seeping between my thighs.

I can't wait to have him inside of me.

"*Bel.*" Liam rewards my efforts with a satisfying growl. "You're doing amazing. God, I never fucking knew it could feel like this." His hips pump as he clutches my ponytail like reins. "You sexy fucking thing. Your mouth was created for sinning. Sinning with me." He gives a particular hard thrust that sends more than half of him inside my mouth. I gag. He looks apologetic for two seconds, but his darker, lustier side wins. "Please. Open wider. Let me slide more of my cock inside of you. I need this, baby. Need you. Yes, that's it. That's it. Do it again. Again. Again." He lets out vile curses when I relax my jaw and let him have at it. "Fuck, you're perfect."

His heady praise coats my organs like warm honey. I feel triumphant, empowered, and in total control even though I'm the one kneeling on the bed, getting my mouth railed by his dick. I peer up at him with a kittenish gleam. Liam stares down at me, breathing harshly as he thrusts away like this is the first and last blow job of his life.

My heart's fluttering like a restless bird locked in a cage.

I savour every stuttered groan escaping him, just as he savours every noise I concoct while choking on his dick. It's beautiful really. A choir of salaciousness.

Liam's dick feels like it swells even bigger than ever. Just when I think he's about to erupt, he yanks out with a sloshing sound.

"Are you okay?" He heaves and wipes away my tears.

I cough and nod, proud of myself for actually having been able to take him. "W-Why did you stop?"

Liam takes hold of his dick again—thicker, harder, and redder than ever—and jerks twice, gritting his teeth. He looks like he's in pain. "I want to finish inside you," he pleads raggedly. "I need to feel your tight pussy wrapped around my cock, *mo chroí.*"

I take the scrunchie out of my hair and shake out my black strands before moving backwards on the bed. I'm burning with heat and every emotion feels heightened. "I need to feel you inside of me too."

Liam climbs onto the bed with me and reaches into his nightstand for a condom. "You will." He tears the foil packet with his teeth. "I promise, you will in a minute."

I steal the condom from him, then roll it over his cock and give it a quick squeeze. God was not playing when he created my man. He's huge and perfect and I'm enamoured. "Go slow, okay? Just in the beginning so I can get used to you."

Planting his forearms on either side of my head, Liam nods and kisses my eyes, murmuring soft praise. Thanking me for giving him the pleasure of my mouth. Thanking me for simply existing. And as I lie underneath him, tears burning the back of my lids, I wonder if any woman has ever felt as revered as I do in this moment.

It's on the tip of my tongue to tell him I love him so much, but Liam steals the air in my lungs by giving me a gamely kiss.

"Liam?" I whisper into our lip-lock.

"Yes?" he whispers back.

"Spank my ass and pull my hair when you fuck me." I bite his bottom lip and tug. "I want to feel completely owned by you tonight."

Those blue eyes of his darken with something menacing and he groans. "If you keep talking like that, I'm going to come in three seconds and this will be over before it begins."

I wink. "Good. Come as fast as you want. We have all night."

CHAPTER 12

Liam

None of my fantasies can compare to the real thing.

With the love of my life lying beneath me, bratty smirk, rosy cheeks, and her tan skin covered in a sheen of sweat. She's delectable with all her soft skin and curves.

And I'm spellbound by her.

I comb my fingers through her hair as we gaze into each other's eyes. "We have forever," I correct, planting a kiss to the tip of her nose. "The rest of our lives."

My chest tightens when she stares up at me with so much love. "Yes, we do."

All my doubts and worries about this moment fade away. There's not a scrap of insecurity in me as I palm her waist and hips, tucking her lower body closer to mine. This stunning nymph of a woman has given me the honour of making love to her, and I'm going to make this the most memorable night of our lives.

A shudder of bliss wracks through me as I position my cock between her wet slit, rocking tightly against her folds. I'm bigger in comparison, but if there's one strong woman who can take me—and enjoy it too—it's Bel. "Hold on to me, baby."

Mabel grasps my shoulders and glances at the spot where we are nearly joined. The obscene sight beckons us.

My cockhead grazes her opening. I hear her inhale and the need to be completely connected to her—mind, body, and soul—overwhelms me.

123

Locking our lips together, I thrust my cock home, absorbing Mabel's sensual cry.

The thundering of my heart drowns out my groan and her responding, "Liam!"

Sheer rhapsody pulses through my veins, slithers down my spine, and clenches my balls. I've never felt anything so glorious in my life. Making love to Mabel is a spiritual experience that shakes me to my core. Too much and yet not enough. I'm as whole as I am undone.

This girl, she's forever altered me.

I'll never be the same again.

"*Mo ghrá?*" My love, I call to her in my mother tongue, panting, "Have I hurt you?"

"No," she sobs with pleasure, squeezing me with her cunt. "I'm feeling..."

She can't complete the sentence. She doesn't need to. I know exactly what she means to say.

"I'm feeling it too, Bel," I murmur, taking her mouth in a long kiss drenched with my devotion.

We fit so well together, it's madness. For one human to be so perfectly and wretchedly yours that losing them would ruin you forever.

Mabel is irrevocably mine and I'll fight anyone for trying to change that.

"I can't take it anymore," she pleads, wrenching her lips from mine. They're red and puffy from my ministrations. "Give it to me, Liam. Fuck me hard."

Queen of my heart, I can never deny her.

She owns me.

And in this moment, I own her too.

Mabel Garcia is the next beat of my heart and the very breath travelling through my lungs, giving me life.

Slowly, I withdraw my cock and we both huff, watching her slick pussy coat and grip me magnificently.

"You're so fucking hot, baby." I barely recognize my guttural voice. My hands hook beneath her knees and push her thighs to her chest, folding her in half. Her pretty toes rest on my shoulders. I have the urge to suck them. "You've been keeping this cunt tight and ready for your man, eh?" I rock inside of her, savouring her clench. "You knew once I got my hands on you, I'd be putting this sexy body in every position for the next hour." I pull out and thrust back harder this time, causing her entire body to quake. She moans louder than ever. "We're going to take our time tonight." *Thrust.* "I'm going to fuck you hard like the bad girl you are until you're dripping in sweat." *Thrust. Thrust.* "Until you can't think past the way I'm working this supermodel pussy." *Thrust. Thrust. Thrust.* "Until you're screaming my name from how good I've got you coming around my cock." *Thrust. Thrust. Thrust. Thrust.* "You with me, sweetheart?"

She's moaning her agreement, fingers twisting in my sheets, lips shaped in an 'O,' tits bouncing at my growing, rough pace.

The erotic picture fuels my fervour.

I start to fuck her *hard.* Just like she asked.

My girlfriend is loving every second of it.

"Liam," Mabel whines when my thumb starts playing with her clit in time with my measured pumps. I'm doing my best not to cede control and go all *poundtown* on her. "You're stretching my pussy full and fucking it so good—Ahhh!"

Her praise drives me crazy. I shift her legs so they wrap around my waist and bear down on her, going faster. "Beg for it," I snarl, biting her jaw. "Beg me to make you come."

"Please, Liam!" she chokes out, raking her fingers down my back. "Pleasepleaseplease."

The room is ringing with the sound of my headboard banging against the wall, our sweaty hips and stomachs smacking against each other, and our groans as I hammer in her creaming pussy. The scent of arousal clings in the air and ignites a roguish intensity that has my big body fortressing hers, my fists knotting in her hair, and my mouth at her ear as I whisper dirty things to the love of my life.

None of those boys were doing it for you, huh? You needed a real man to treat this cunt. Give it a nice pounding. The kind that makes you lose the ability to walk the next day.

One fuck and you're already addicted. Look at you, working your hips to cram every last inch of my cock. Begging for me like you'll die without this.

I've got your number, baby. You want me to spank your pussy while telling you you're the prettiest girl I've ever seen. You want me to compliment you and debase you at the same time. You want me to kiss you like I adore you, but fuck you like I despise you.

"Oh my God!" She goes buck wild, holding on to me like I'm her anchor. "I'm right there!"

I can feel her pussy rippling around my cock and it's incredible. I groan, laying a sloppy kiss to her panting mouth. "I know, baby. Come for me. I want to see you coming."

Mabel is even more beautiful in the midst of orgasm. Face flushed, shiny skin, eyes half-mast, and lips echoing the most sinful noises, she falls apart in my arms with a final shout of my name. "*Liam!*"

"We're not done yet, sunshine." I fight my impending release as I pull out of Mabel's spasming pussy. She gasps at the loss of me before I'm flipping her around, ass up, face down and entering her from behind. "Not until your ass is bearing my handprints."

Wet heat engulfs me once more. This time I'm even deeper, my cock hitting her back wall with every drive. I push and she takes, her body blooming open like a pretty flower. Mabel's face is in my pillow as she wails, backing her bouncing ass into my lap for *more, more, more* because she's such a greedy girl. She can't be satisfied with three orgasms. No. She needs an all-nighter where she wakes up in the morning completely sore and dotted with love bites.

My left hand delves into her hair and jerks her head up, causing her spine to arch beautifully and for my heavy balls to slap against her clit with every fast, rearing thrust. Nonsensical, pornographic sounds escape her lips, a mixture of half cries, half moans. "*Sogoodsogoodsogood.*"

"Horny tight vixen, you're loving this first-time fuck, aren't you?" I growl, her right ass cheek bearing the brunt of four consecutive spanks. Her backside slams into my flexing belly with every thrust and I can tell she's near. Again. "Who would have known my sweet pen pal would be such a slut in bed?" My sweat drips onto her back and my fingers dig into her hips like half-moons. "Your secret's safe with me." I rain kisses over her back until I reach her ear and whisper, "Sexy model by day and Liam's dirty fuck toy by night." There's no rhythm now. Pure carnal lust has me *thrusthrusthrusting* so jarringly, her cries turn mute and her expression morphs into euphoria. "Now be a good girl and scream my name when you come. I want the neighbours to know I'm the only guy who gets the privilege of fucking you, baby."

Mabel looks over her shoulder. Seeing her heart in her eyes, a dam breaks inside of me. I don't just see the words—the prominent *I love you*—I feel it in her gaze. It's in mine, too.

Helplessly, I kiss her as I push us towards the edge.

We lose ourselves in our passion. Nothing matters besides *us* and this bond woven through ink-stained letters filled with heartfelt confessions.

My girl screams my name, flooding my cock like a waterfall.

I come with her, muffling my roar in her sweaty neck. "*Bel*."

I might as well have lost consciousness after that powerful climax. I don't remember how I withdrew from her embrace, how I disposed of the condom, and how I found myself lying on my back, regaining my breathing, as a lush, sated Mabel lies curled by my side, half draped over me, caressing my beard and drawing invisible hearts on my torso.

"Liam?" Mabel murmurs.

I turn my head and press a kiss to her forehead. "Hm?"

"That was amazing."

I grin, my heart beating fast. "I know."

"I want to do it again."

"Give me a few minutes to rest up and I'll get it up again, you sex monster."

"I'm going to ride you reverse cowgirl this time."

I draw my fingers up her arm in a caress. "Sounds good to me."

"Liam?"

"Hm?"

"I love you," she says shyly.

A myriad of emotions steamrolls through me. I knew it, felt it, and saw it coming. But hearing it all the same feels like I've won the biggest trophy—this girl's love and affection.

Mabel is used to my silence, but right now she needs words and more importantly, I *need* her to hear them. Wrapping my arms around her more firmly, I draw her into my embrace.

Wordlessly, Mabel nuzzles the scar on my cheek.

I press a kiss to the crown of her head and give her my confession.

"For a long time, my life was laced with shadows. I was accustomed to darkness, but then you fell into my life. You were like the sun. You brought me light and suddenly, I didn't know how to live without your beacon." I cup her cheek and tilt her face to meet my gaze. "You became my home—a safe place for my dreams and hopes to thrive—and I couldn't imagine my world without you in it. Your existence brings me so much abundance, I can't even put it into words, Bel." I kiss her forehead when her eyes glaze over. "You're not just my best friend or my girlfriend. You're the other half of me." I finally kiss her lips, tasting happiness, tears, and sunshine. "And I promise you, for as long as we live, I'm going to cherish you and spoil you rotten until the end of time. Because I love you, Mabel. You're it for me. You're my girl. Always and forever."

"Oh, Liam. You're the other half of me too." Mabel's smile is watery. She rests her forehead on mine. "I promise to support you, love you, and be there for you. Always and forever. And just know that you and me? We're going to live the best life filled with laughter, joy, and epic adventures."

My own eyes sting when she finishes.

This beautiful soul.

I weave our fingers together and press a kiss to her knuckles, specifically the finger where she's going to wear my ring one day. "I can't wait, babe."

She smiles.

I smile back.

Mabel Garcia is no longer my fantasy.

She's my reality.

EPILOGUE

Mabel

A few years later...

Liam and I are headed on a road trip to Mystic Falls, Virginia—aka Covington, Georgia—to celebrate our five-year anniversary.

"Do we have everything we need, *mo ghrá?*"

Years later and that term of endearment never fails to melt my heart. Nothing makes me feel more adored than Liam whispering sweet little words in his mother tongue when we touch.

"Yup." I settle into the passenger's seat of Liam's car and buckle my seat belt. I've checked our bags about three times to ensure we didn't forget anything. "We've got everything, *Bob*."

Liam shoves a teasing hand into the nape of my neck to tickle me. His crawling fingers go from my shoulders to my waist and I'm reduced to a laughing fit before I manage to bat his hand away. My boyfriend acts like he doesn't like the nickname, but the smile nestled in his beard says otherwise.

"Smart-ass," he teases.

"You love me," I retort.

Liam sighs and pins me with a soft look. "Yeah, I do."

We grin at each other and share a secret look. The kind that says 'Even after years, you remain my favourite thing on this planet.'

As road trip tradition calls, we make a pit stop to grab breakfast—coffees and bagels—and then we're off to our destination.

In the last half decade of us dating, Liam and I have travelled together often. Ireland. The Philippines. Italy. Mexico. And loads of places within North America via road trips. You can say we both have a serious case of wanderlust and the scratch world map in my room is a testament to that. We've made a pact to visit at least half of the Earth by the time we turn seventy.

I'd say our plans are going pretty well so far.

My phone buzzes with a text message.

Have a safe trip, May. Text me when you reach there. xo — Ken

Will do. I love you and I'll see you when I return. <3 —May

Don't forget to bring me back a souvenir! —Ken

I'll bring you back some vervain. —May

LOL perfect! —Ken

Kennedy and I remain close even after graduating from Vesta University's business school. She's still one of my ride-or-dies and I adore her to pieces. Currently, she's climbing the corporate ladder and living happily ever after with the love of her life.

As for me, my modelling career really kicked off after my undergrad. I've been booked and busy for three years with endorsements, photoshoots, and runways. I thought the solo travelling for work would put a strain on my relationship with Liam, but we've found ways to make even the occasional long-distance work. Doesn't matter where I am, though, because I always come back home to my Liam.

I spend a lot more time in Montardor now that I'm working closely with Maison Sereno, a Canadian designer brand founded by one of my university friends.

I'm also getting to put my business degree to use now that I'm about to launch my own skincare line in a few months. Liam convinced me a year ago to take the leap and transform my passion for beauty into another income stream.

I can't wait to see what the future has in store for us.

Liam has done pretty amazing for himself too. He's officially an engineer, the Iron Ring on his finger another proof of his accomplishment. He's worked on several projects, but his favourite ones remain the jobs he does in our home.

Since buying a nice bungalow last year, Liam has built us a gazebo in the backyard, a big birdhouse for the cardinals that visit us in the warmer seasons, a walk-in closet that doubles up as my vanity room, a sex dungeon in our basement for our newfound kinky streak, and the list goes on.

He never ceases to amaze me or make me proud with everything he does.

Liam notices me glancing at him from the passenger's side. He turns his head for a few seconds, a ghost of a smile on his lips. "What are you thinking?"

He never admits it out loud, but he loves when I just gaze at him in marvel.

"That you look good enough to eat."

After all this time, he still grabs my hand when he's driving to pepper my knuckles with sweet kisses. "Oh, I know."

Safe to say, over the span of five years, Liam has grown in confidence and embraced all the pieces that compose his beauty. I'm so happy to have witnessed the work he's put into respecting and accepting his whole being. Self-love looks wonderful on him.

"You look good enough to eat too."

I give him a knowing expression. "Two hours until our next en route stop and I'm fully banking on you keeping that promise."

A full-belly laugh erupts from him. He's used to my humour by now. "Deal."

We enter the highway and I surf through my Spotify until I find what I'm looking for.

Liam & Mabel's playlist.

Soft RnB filters through the car and our hands tighten together, listening to old and new songs that are reminiscent of our relationship.

I notice the GPS reroutes us. "What's going on?"

"We just need to make one more quick stop."

"Where?"

"It's a surprise." He rubs my bare thigh in comfort. "Don't worry, you're going to like this."

"Can I get a hint?"

"No, but I want you to do me a favour."

I cross my legs and quirk an eyebrow. "Shoot."

"In exactly thirty seconds, I want you to close your eyes and only open them when I tell you."

133

"Okay," I drawl, confused.

Liam shakes his head. "It won't be for long, I promise. I wanted to bring a blindfold, but that would ruin your makeup and leave you unhappy so…"

"Good call." I laugh. "Okay, I'm excited about whatever this is."

Giddiness unfurling in the pit of my stomach, I close my eyes with a deep breath and lean the side of my head against the window. Moments pass in companionable silence with a gentle love ballad murmuring in the background.

The car rolls to a stop.

Curiosity nearly has me peeking one eye open to cheat, but Liam wants to surprise me and I give him that courtesy.

Maybe we're stopping by the florist to grab a bouquet of sunflowers? Although that doesn't make much sense, considering the blooms will wither away during our drive to Mystic Falls.

I hear Liam turning off the car, unbuckling his seat belt, and opening and closing his door. He's rounding the car, I know, because he never lets me open my own door. Such a gentleman, this one.

My door clicks open and Liam says, "Keep your eyes closed."

"I will," I mock-grumble as he unbuckles my belt and hauls me out of my seat. I have to hold on to him so I don't fall. Except if I ever fell, Liam would always catch me.

"Your eyes are still closed?"

"If you ask me one more time, Bob, I'm opening them and ruining this entire thing."

He slaps my ass. "Fucking brat."

"What are you going to do about it?"

"Renege on my promise to eat you out in the back seat of my car. I even brought your pink sparkly dildo this time, so that will really suck for you."

I pout.

He kisses my glossed lips. "Follow me."

Braiding our fingers together, he walks us forward. We're outdoors, given the heat of the sun, the sound of chirping birds, and the grass prickling my open toes. In the distance, I hear water.

"We're here." Liam releases my hands and comes to stand behind me, kissing my cheek. "Open your eyes."

When I do, I see the picturesque landscape of our spot. Blue summer sky. Rippling water. A flock of birds flying. Trees rustling overhead with the gentle breeze. The bench where we first confessed our feelings rests next to us.

"It's even more beautiful during the day, eh?" Smiling, I spin around. "What are we doing here—oh my God!"

The remainder of my words dies in my throat when I catch my beautiful warrior kneeling before me with a small velvet box in his hands.

A bright yellow diamond ring winks in the sunlight.

I gasp. "Liam…"

He takes my free hand and lays it against his chest, over his thumping heart. "Mabel Lani Garcia, you're my best friend and my soul mate. Every single day, I count my lucky stars that you and I found our way to each other through those first letters. Because the truth is, I don't know what I would do without you. You make me smile, you make me laugh, and you make me feel like our life is one big adventure that's only just begun. I love you with my entire heart and I want to spend the rest of my life with you. Marry me, sweetheart. Say yes and make me the happiest man to have walked this earth."

Between that heartfelt speech, a single tear escapes me. "I-I…Oh my God, Liam."

He kisses my palm and I belatedly notice the sheen of moisture in his blue eyes. They're shining with so much love. For me. Always for me. "Say yes, Bel."

I laugh, but the sound is watery. "Yes! Yes, I'll marry you, Liam!"

The engagement ring is slipped onto my finger. I don't have a chance to admire it before Liam is rising to his full six-foot-five height and clasping my face to kiss me breathless.

"Just so you know, I want a big destination wedding," I murmur once we pull away.

Liam O'Connell presses his forehead to mine and says with an epic smile, "I'll always give you anything you want, Mabel."

The End

ACKNOWLEDGEMENTS

Thank you so much for taking a chance on *The Guy For Me!* I sincerely hope you enjoyed reading about Mabel and Liam. Their story was such a treat to write and I'm looking forward to sharing more novellas in the future with you all!

As always, this project could not have been completed without the help and support of so many amazing individuals.

To Annie and Armita, thank you for alpha reading *The Guy For Me*. You both are such an integral part of my publishing process and I could not imagine doing this without you. From brainstorming, to writing the first draft, to going over edits, to wrapping up the final product, and to every other little thing in between, you're always there to give me feedback and encouragement when I need it most. I'm extremely lucky to have you in my life. I know I sound like a broken record, but I love you with all my heart and you mean the world to me. Thank you for existing and being some of the most amazing people I've ever met.

To Alicia, Emma, Ellie, and Marie, thank you so much for beta reading! The insight you ladies provided really helped me see the manuscript in a new light and tweak it to perfection! I'm very privileged to have such kind souls like you in my circle, and I'm super grateful that our paths crossed when they did. Meeting you all really feels like fate. I love you times infinity.

To my sweet friend Paula, thank you for reading this novella on such short notice and helping me with the Tagalog lines. It truly means a lot to me that you took the time out of your busy schedule to do this! In case I haven't said it already, I appreciate and love you!

To my lovely editor Emily, it's our third time working together on a project and it certainly won't be our last. You're always so thorough with editing and I always learn something new from you. You're the best and I adore you!

To the cover designing team at Qamber Designs (especially Naj and Tima), thank you for creating such a beautiful cover and for meeting my vision! I really appreciate your expertise and patience throughout this entire process. The final product is so gorgeous and I still can't stop staring at it!

To my interior formatter Nada, you've worked your magic once more and created another masterpiece! It's always such a pleasure teaming up with you, and I'm constantly in awe of your talent and kindness throughout these projects. Thank you for always being so wonderful! Can't wait to work together on more future projects!

To Candi from Candi Kane PR, thank you for all your assistance with this release!

To Mom, thank you for praying for me, being my biggest supporter, and for always believing in my dreams. I truly believe I've come this far because of all your blessings. I love you forever.

To the wonderful ladies from bookstagram (Eden, Ellen, Chiara, Himani, Leah, Maxine, Meena, Niss, Sahra, Sasha, Smiqa, Salma, Ria, Yas, Youssra, Zahra, and so many more), thank you for cheering me on and being so very kind. I adore you!

And lastly, to my beautiful readership, my queens, thank you for your constant support over the years. As it's been said before, I love you to the moon and back. Always. <3.

If you enjoyed reading *The Guy For Me*, I would really appreciate it if you took the time to leave a rating and review on Amazon and Goodreads. It's a huge help to indie authors and I'm looking forward to hearing your thoughts!

Love always,

Marzy

ABOUT THE AUTHOR

Marzy Opal is a romance author who writes steamy and swoon-worthy romances. Her stories always contain dirty-talking heroes, empowered heroines, everlasting love, and lots of spice. Aside from writing, Marzy has a strong passion for lattes, entrepreneurship, women empowerment and leadership!

CONNECT WITH ME

Enjoyed *The Guy For Me*? Make sure to stay connected for upcoming books and series! My social media handles are @marzyopal and you can find me on:
Goodreads | Instagram | Facebook | Marzy's Queens Readers' Facebook Group | Pinterest | Spotify | TikTok | Twitter
www.marzyopal.com